TOM FAIRFIELD'S SCHOOLDAYS

BY

ALLEN CHAPMAN

TOM FAIRFIELD'S SCHOOLDAYS

CHAPTER I

TOM HEARS STRANGE NEWS

"Hi, Tom, give us a ride in your boat; will you?"

"Take us across to the other side of the river."

The request and the suggestion came from two lads who were walking toward a small boathouse, on the edge of a rather wide river. The youth to whom they spoke looked up from a small motorboat, the engine of which he was cleaning.

"What do you want to go over to the other side of the river for, Dick Jones?" asked Tom Fairfield, of the lad who had made that suggestion.

"Got to go on an errand for dad, and it's too far to walk away around by the bridge. Take me over, will you?"

"I will if I can get this engine to run."

"What's the matter with it?" asked Will Bennett, the companion of Dick Jones. The two were chums, and friends of Tom Fairfield, all of them living in the village of Briartown. Tom, whose parents were quite well off, had recently bought a motorboat, not very large, but of sufficient size to enable him to take out several of his chums. "What's the matter with the engine?" asked Will again, as he and his chum walked out on the small dock, at the end of which the motorboat was made fast.

"Matter with it? What isn't the matter with it?" asked Tom in some disgust. "The cylinder is flooded with oil, that's what's the matter, and I don't know how many more things I'll find wrong before I get through. It's all that Dent Wilcox's fault."

"How's that?" asked Dick, as he and his chum watched Tom trying to drain some of the lubricating oil out through a small valve.

"Oh, I took Dent out for a ride last night, and as I was in a hurry to get up to the house when I got back, I asked him to shut off the oil cups. But it's like everything else he does—he's too lazy, almost, to breathe. He didn't turn off the oil, and all that was in the cups ran into the cylinder during the night. I've tried for the last half hour to get the engine started, but she won't run."

"That's too bad," spoke Will sympathetically.

"I'll never trust Dent to do anything for me again," went on Tom. "I ought to have seen to the oil cups myself, and I will next time. Wait until I catch him!"

"There he goes now!" exclaimed Dick, pointing to a lad crossing a field some distance away. "Shall I run and tell him you want to see him?"

"No, it isn't worth while," replied Tom. "Besides, he's so lazy he wouldn't walk down here. But I'll talk to him like a Dutch Uncle when I do see him. Now let's see if the engine will work. If it does, I'll give you fellows a ride."

Once more Tom turned the flywheel over several times, but, though the engine coughed, wheezed and spluttered, as though in apology at having such poor health, it did not start.

"Say, you haven't got your forward switch on!" suddenly exclaimed Will. "There's no spark."

"No wonder!" cried Tom. "I remember now, I had it on, and then, as I didn't want to get a shock when I was cleaning the spark plug, I shut it off. Then I forgot to put it on again. Hop in, and close the switch, Will, and then maybe we can start. I guess most of the oil is out, now."

The two chums got in the boat, and Will, making his way forward, closed the connection. Then Tom, who had remained near the motor, again turned over the flywheel. This time there was an explosion, and the engine worked rapidly. The propeller churned the water, and the painter strained as the boat moved forward.

"Hurray!" cheered Dick.

"That's the stuff!" exclaimed Will, at the prospect of a ride.

"Yes, I guess it's all right now," assented Tom. He shut off the engine by pulling out a switch near it, and added: "Wait until I get some more oil from the boathouse, and I'll be with you."

As Tom started up the dock toward the little building, which he had built, with the help of his chums, to house his boat, he saw, coming along the road that ran near the river, a young man in a small auto runabout. The youth was well dressed, but on his face was a look of sadness and worry, in contrast, Tom thought, to the cheerful expression he should have worn.

"If I had a natty little car like that, I wouldn't look so glum," reasoned Tom, as he opened the boathouse door. The runabout came nearer, and the lone occupant of it, bringing it to a stop opposite Tom, called out:

"Is there any place around here where I can hire a boat for a row of an hour or so?"

"Not near here," replied Tom.

The young man's eyes rested on Tom's own trim rowing craft.

"Is that one to hire?" he asked, nodding toward it.

"No," replied our hero. "But if you'd like to take it I've no objections. I've got a motorboat, and, if you like, I'll take you for a ride in that. Did you want to go anywhere in particular?"

"No, I just want to get off by myself, and worry over my troubles," and the newcomer laughed, but the laugh had no merriment in it.

"Troubles?" questioned Tom, now that the other had given him an opening. "You don't look as if you had troubles."

"Well, I have—lots of 'em. I've acted like a blamed chump, and now I've got to pay the piper. A man is trying to make trouble for me, and I guess he'll succeed, all right. I'm too easy, that's the trouble. But I'm not going to bother you with my woes."

"Do you want to come for a ride with me?" asked Tom. "I'm going to take a couple of friends across the river."

"No, thank you. I don't want to seem stiff, but really I'd be better off by myself for a time. So, if you really mean it, and will lend me your boat, I'll go for a row alone. I was out on a little country run—I live in Camden—and when I saw this river, looking so calm and peaceful, I just felt as though I'd like to row on it, and forget my troubles."

"You may take the boat, and welcome," went on Tom, looking at the other, and forming a liking for him at once.

"Thanks. My name is Bennington—Bruce Bennington. I haven't a card, or I'd give you one."

"My name's Tom Fairfield," spoke our hero, and the two shook hands.

"Know how to row?" asked Tom, as the newcomer started toward where the small boat was moored.

"Yes, I'm on the crew at Elmwood Hall. I'm a senior there," Bruce explained.

"Oh!" exclaimed Tom, for he had often heard of that place of learning. "That's quite a school," he added. "I've often wished I could go there."

"Yes, it's quite a place," admitted Bruce Bennington. "And we have a pretty fair crew. You won't want your boat right away?"

"No. And the reason I asked if you could row was because there are some stiff currents in the river. You're welcome to come in the motorboat if you like, though it isn't much of a craft."

"No, thank you, I'd rather row off by myself, and do some good hard thinking. I've got to go back to school as soon as the fall term opens, which will be in about two weeks, and I'd like to find a way out of my troubles before then, if I can."

"It's too bad," spoke Tom sympathetically, for he had, somehow, come to form a strange and sudden liking for this lad. Tom looked into the other's frank and pleasant face, and really wished he could help him.

"Well, I guess I'll have to squirm out of it the best I can," went on Bruce. "A good row, and a rest in the cool shadows, will calm me down, maybe, and I'll try to make some plans before I have to get back to the grind. I'll take good care of your boat."

By the manner in which he entered it, and took up the oars, Tom saw that Bruce knew how to handle the craft. The auto runabout had been left near the dock, and a little later the senior was sculling down the stream.

"Who was that?" asked Tom's chums, as he rejoined them.

He explained briefly, as he filled the empty oil cups, and soon he and the two lads were puffing across the river in the motorboat. The rowing craft had disappeared around a bend in the stream.

"Troubles, eh?" mused Will. "I don't believe I'd let much trouble me if I went to a cracker-jack school like Elmwood Hall, and had a runabout like that."

"Me either," added Dick.

"Well, you never can tell," spoke Tom, as he thought of the sad look on the senior's face—a look that had returned several times during the talk, in spite of the frequent smiles. "He seems like a nice sort of chap."

"Did he say what his trouble was?" asked Will.

"No, and I didn't ask him. Said some man had it in for him. Look out where you're steering, Dick."

"Why, what's the matter?" asked Dick, who had requested Tom to let him take the wheel for a time.

"There's a big rock somewhere out here," went on the owner of the motorboat. "I must mark it with a buoy, or I'll hit it myself some night. Keep more to the left."

Dick spun the wheel over, and the boys rode on, talking of many things.

"Where do you think you'll go to school this fall?" asked Will of Tom.

"Oh, back to the Academy, I suppose."

"Why, you graduated from there in June!"

"I know I did, but there's going to be a post-graduate class formed, I hear. Going to take up first year college work, and dad talks of sending me. I wish I could go to Elmwood Hall, though, or some place like that."

"So do I!" cried Will.

"Boarding school's the place!" affirmed Dick, with energy. "I'd like to go to one."

They had reached the other side of the river now and Dick Jones, who had been sent by his father to take a message to a lumberman, started off on his errand, Will and Tom promising to wait for him in the motorboat. When Dick returned on the run, Tom yielded to the request of the two lads, and took them for a run up the stream.

"That is, unless you have something to do, Tom," spoke Will.

"No, I'm going to have all the fun I can before school opens, that's all. And it will do the engine good to run a bit and get rid of the oil that chump Dent let run in."

The boys were out in the motorboat for about two hours, and, on nearing the dock on the return trip, Dick remarked:

"That fellow's auto is gone."

"Is my boat there?" asked Tom, who was tinkering with the motor of his craft.

"Yes," replied Will, who was steering.

"All right; I guess that fellow got tired of rowing, or maybe he thought of a way out of his troubles, and came in."

When Tom had made fast his motorboat, he went to the rowing craft to see if it was in good condition. He saw a piece of paper on one of the seats, held down by a little stone. Picking it up he read:

"Many thanks for the use of your boat. I had a fine row, and I feel better, though I'm as much up a tree as ever. I hope to see you again, sometime. If ever you are near Elmwood Hall, look me up.

"BRUCE BENNINGTON."

"That was nice of him," remarked Will, as Tom showed him the note.

"And he didn't damage your boat any," spoke Dick.

"No, he knows how to handle 'em—he rows on the Elmwood Hall crew," said Tom. "Well, so long, fellows. I'm going for a long run to-morrow, if you'd like to come."

"Sure!" they chorused.

But Tom was not destined to take that long run on the morrow, for, when he reached his home, not far from the river, he heard strange tidings, that made quite a difference in his plans.

As Tom entered the house he saw his father holding a letter, that he had evidently been reading to his wife, and discussing with her. There was a look of concern on the faces of Mr. and Mrs. Brokaw Fairfield.

"What's the matter?" asked Tom, quickly. "Any bad news?"

"No, not exactly bad news, Tom," replied his father. "But it is news, and it's going to make quite a difference to us—to you also."

"What is it?"

"You remember that property in Australia, Tom, which was left to me by an uncle; don't you?" asked Mr. Fairfield.

"Yes," replied our hero, for he had often heard the inheritance mentioned. "What about it?"

"Well, I've been trying to dispose of it, and have the money from the sale sent to me here, but it seems that some trouble has arisen, and I've got to go there to straighten it out. I tried to do it by correspondence, but I have just received a letter from a lawyer in Sydney, saying that my personal presence is needed, or I may lose it all. So—"

"Your father and I have decided to go to Australia!" suddenly broke in Mrs. Fairfield, anxious to get the worst over. "Oh, Tom, I don't want to go at all, and leave you behind, but I've got to!"

"What!" cried Tom. "Can't I go? You two going to Australia, and leaving me alone here? Oh, say, now—"

"Wait, Tom," cautioned his father with a smile, "we're not going to leave you alone, exactly. Besides, there is your education to think of, and we may be gone for many months."

"Oh, but I say—" began Tom again.

"Now, dear son," began his mother in a gentle voice, "we have it all planned out for you. You are to go to boarding school while we are away."

"Boarding school!" Tom's eyes began to sparkle. After all, this might be as good as going to Australia.

"Yes," said his father, "and we have picked out—"

"Elmwood Hall!" broke in Mrs. Fairfield, unable to let her husband tell all the news.

"Elmwood Hall!" cried Tom, thinking of the note in his pocket from Bruce Bennington.

"Yes," spoke Mr. Fairfield, "though if you'd rather go to some other place it may be arranged. But your mother and I picked out Elmwood Hall, and—"

"Elmwood Hall!" cried Tom again. "Say, that's all right. I'm satisfied! That beats Australia. When are you going? When can I start for Elmwood? Have you got a catalog from there? Say, I've got something to tell you!" and Tom, overcoming a desire to stand on his head, pulled out the note Bruce had left in his boat.

"Elmwood Hall!" exclaimed Tom again. "This is the best ever!"

CHAPTER II

THE DRIFTING BOAT

"What makes you so enthusiastic about Elmwood Hall, Tom?" asked Mr. Fairfield, when his son had somewhat calmed down. "I didn't know you knew much about it."

"I don't except what I've heard and read, but it just happens that I met a fellow from there to-day." And Tom told of his talk with Bruce Bennington, showing his parents the letter.

"Hum, that is rather odd," spoke Mr. Fairfield. "I wonder what his trouble could have been? Bennington—Bennington. I've heard that name before. Oh, I know; Mr. Bennington is a millionaire manufacturer. That must be his son, though if he's in trouble I should think Mr. Bennington would help him out."

"Maybe it isn't money," spoke Tom. "But, anyhow, I'm glad I'm going to Elmwood, and maybe I'll get chummy with Bruce Bennington, though there's not much chance, for he's a Senior, and I'll be a Freshman."

"I hope, if you can, that you'll help him," said Mrs. Fairfield. "And oh, Tom, do you think they'll haze you?"

"If they do, I guess I can stand it," replied her son. "Everyone has to be hazed. I won't mind. But now tell me something about going to Australia."

"It's going to be quite a trip," said Mr. Fairfield, "and one I wish I could get out of, but I can't. We'll start as soon as we can, Tom. We're to go to San Francisco by train, and take a steamer there. I'll write at once, and make arrangements for you to go to Elmwood Hall. Your mother will see to getting what clothes you need. Here is a catalog of the school."

Tom eagerly looked the pamphlet over, while his father went to his library to write some letters and Mrs. Fairfield, not without some misgivings as to what might happen to Tom at boarding school, or to herself and her husband on their long trip, went to look over her son's wardrobe.

As I have explained, Mr. Fairfield was quite well off, and had the prospect of more wealth. He did not care to lose his Australian inheritance, and, though the journey meant some trouble for him, in that it would complicate his business affairs at home, he decided to make it. He had long promised his wife a trip abroad and now was the chance for it, as they intended to come home by way of Europe.

Tom Fairfield was a tall, well built youth, fond of all out-doors sports, and about as lively a lad as you would care to meet.

He had lived in Briartown all his life, though he had traveled extensively with his father and mother, and knew considerable of the world. He was an only son, a sister having died when a little girl.

Tom had many friends in the village, where his father's silk factory was located, and our hero took part in the scenes and activities of the place. He had attended the Academy there, and was one of the best football and baseball players. He always had a liking for the water, and since getting his motorboat, had been on Pine river more often than ever. He had tried to get up a crew at the Academy, but could not seem to interest enough boys, or get them to subscribe the necessary funds.

Tom had one or two enemies, too, chiefly because he would not let them bully him, but they did not worry him, for any lad of spirit is as likely to have enemies as friends, and Tom had plenty of the latter.

"Jove! To think that I'm really going to Elmwood Hall!" Tom whispered to himself, as he leafed over the catalog, and looked at the pictures of the various buildings. "That'll be great! I wish I knew some of the fellows who were going there, but I guess I can soon get acquainted. I wonder if I can pass the entrance examinations?"

He looked at the requirements for the Freshman class, and noted that there was no study but what he had had at the Academy.

"I guess I can do it," he said.

There were soon busy days in the Fairfield household.

Besides making arrangements for the voyage, and getting their business affairs in shape to leave, Mr. and Mrs. Fairfield had to arrange for Tom's stay at Elmwood. This was done by correspondence and, about a week after Tom had heard the news, he went to the school to take the entrance examinations. He met a few lads in like case, all rather miserable, and Tom felt a feeling of pride as he walked about the campus, and thought that soon he would be a student there.

"That is, if I pass," he mused. "That Latin exam. was a bit stiff, and so were the maths. Maybe the others will be easier. I hope so, anyhow."

Tom's hopes were realized, for on the second day—the test extending over that time—he had no difficulty in answering the entrance questions. Then he went back home, to receive, a few days later, word that he had passed, and would be admitted to the Freshman class.

"Wow!" he cried, as he read the formal announcement. "That's great! I'm going to tell the boys!"

He rushed off to find Dick and Will, his most particular chums. But, on visiting their houses, he was informed that they had gone fishing on the river.

"I'll find 'em," he said. "I know the fishing hole. I'll go down in my motorboat."

He hurried back to the dock, and, as he reached a point where he could look down to it, he uttered an exclamation of dismay.

"My motorboat!" he cried. "It's gone! Some one has it! If it's stolen—"

He broke into a run, and as he had a good view of the river he saw his boat out in the middle of the stream.

"Well, of all the nerve!" he cried. "Dent Wilcox has taken my boat without asking me. I'll fix him!"

Then he noticed that the boat was not running under her own power, but was drifting down stream.

"Hi there, Dent! What's the matter with you?" Tom cried. "What did you take my boat for? Why don't you start up and run her back here?"

The lazy lad addressed looked up from what was evidently a contemplation of the stalled engine.

"Start her going!" cried Tom. "Start the engine, or you'll be on the rocks!"

"I can't," yelled back Dent. "She's stopped."

"Crank her," ordered Tom. "Turn the flywheel over!"

Dent did so, but in such a lazy and slow fashion that even from shore Tom could see that the lad was not exerting himself enough. The wheel needed a vigorous turn.

"Oh, put some muscle into it!" cried Tom. "You'll never get her going that way!"

"I've tried three or four times, and she won't go," retorted Dent, leaning back against the gunwale, and looking at the engine, as though a mere glance would set it going.

"Keep on trying!" cried Tom. "Don't you see where you're going? You'll be on the rocks in five minutes more! Can't you even steer? Next time you take my boat I'll wallop you good!"

"I didn't think you'd care," came the answer over the stretch of water.

"Well, I do. Now you crank up!"

Dent Wilcox tried again, but his inherent laziness was against him, and nothing resulted. The boat was in the grip of the current, and was rapidly drifting toward the dangerous rocks.

"By Jove! He'll wreck my boat!" thought Tom. "Say!" he cried desperately, "can't you get that engine going somehow, and avoid the rocks?"

"I guess there's no gasolene," retorted Dent.

"Yes, there is, the tank's full."

"Then the batteries have given out."

"Can't be. They're new. Oh, you big chump, to take out my boat when you don't know how to run her!" and Tom looked at his drifting craft in despair.

"Can't you come out and get me?" suggested Dent, as he looked helplessly at the engine.

"Well, of all the nerve!" cried Tom. "But I'll have to, I guess, if I want to save my boat!"

He hurriedly cast off his rowing craft, jumped in, and was soon pulling out toward the drifting motorboat.

CHAPTER III

OFF FOR ELMWOOD HALL

"Talk about lazy fellows!" murmured Tom, as he bent to his oars, "that Dent Wilcox certainly is the limit. He's too lazy to row, so he borrows my motorboat. Then he's too lazy to learn how to crank the engine, and too lazy to turn the flywheel over hard enough. It's a wonder he ever got started, and when he does get going he doesn't take enough pains to look out where he's steering. If he wrecks my boat I'll make him pay for her."

Tom cast a glance over his shoulder toward his craft, and the sight of the boat nearer the rocks made him row faster than ever.

"Why don't you try to steer, or crank her?" he yelled to Dent.

"What's the use?" asked the lazy lad indifferently.

"Use? Lots of use? Do you want to go on the rocks?"

"No, not exactly," spoke Dent, and his voice was quicker than his usual slow tones, as he saw his danger. "But you'll be here in a minute, and you can run things."

"Yes, that's just like you," retorted Tom. "You want someone else to do the work, while you sit around. But I'll make you row back, and pull the boat too, if I can't get her going."

"Oh, Tom, I never could pull this boat back."

"You'll have to," declared our hero grimly, "that is if the engine won't run. Stand by now, to catch my painter."

Dent stood up in the stern of the drifting motorboat, and prepared to catch the line Tom was about to throw to him. Tom was near enough to his motorcraft now so that the headway and the current of the river would carry him to her.

"I hope I can get that engine going," he remarked to himself, as he saw how dangerously near he was to the rocks.

"Catch!" he cried to Dent, throwing the end of his line aboard, and Dent, forgetting his usual lazy habits, made a quick grab for the painter. He reached it, took a turn around a cleat, and in another moment Tom was aboard.

"Pull my rowboat closer up," he ordered Dent. "I'm going to have a try at the motor, and if she doesn't go, we'll have to row out of danger."

He gave a quick look at the engine, and then cried:

"Well, you're a dandy!"

"What's the matter?"

"You didn't have the gasolene turned on."

"I did so. Else how could I have run out from the dock?"

"With what was in the carbureter, of course. But when that was used up, you didn't get any more from the tank. You're a peach to run a motorboat! Don't you ever take mine out again!"

"I won't," murmured Dent, thoroughly ashamed of himself.

With a quick motion Tom turned on the gasolene, saw that the switches were connected, and, with a turn of the flywheel, he had the motor chugging away a second later.

"There you are!" he exclaimed, as he sprang to the steering wheel.

"Glad I don't have to pull in," said Dent, thinking of the work he had escaped.

"Well, it was a narrow squeak," said Tom, as he steered out of the way of the rocks, and then sent his boat around in a graceful curve.

"How'd you come to take my boat?" asked our hero, when he had a chance to collect his thoughts.

"Oh, I just strolled down to the dock, and saw it there. I heard you were out of town—taking the Elmwood Hall examination—and I thought you wouldn't mind."

"I did take the exams., and I passed," spoke Tom, his pride in this rather making him forgive Dent now. "I'll soon be going there to school, and I'll have swell times. I came down to tell Dick and Will that I just got word that I'm to enter the Freshman class, when I saw you had my boat. You want to be more careful after this."

"I will," promised the lazy lad, as he settled himself comfortably on the cushioned seats, and watched Tom steer. The latter, after running ashore, and tying up his rowboat, started for the fishing hole, intending to look for his chums.

"Can't I come along?" asked Dent, who had not offered to get out, nor help Tom tie his boat. "Take me along," he pleaded. "If you go to school I won't get any more rides."

"Well, you have got nerve!" laughed Tom, and yet he felt so elated at the prospect before him that he did not seriously protest. "First you take my boat without permission, then you nearly wreck her, and next you want to have an additional ride. You have your nerve with you, all right."

"Might as well," spoke Dent, lazily, as he lolled back on the cushions. "If you don't ask for things in this world you won't get much."

"I guess that's right," agreed Tom. "You've got more sense than I gave you credit for. But crank that motor now. Let's see if you can get it going. You'll have to work your passage, if you come with me on this voyage."

Dent turned the flywheel over, and after a few attempts he did succeed in getting the engine to go. Then Tom steered down to the fishing hole. Dick and Will saw him coming, and called and waved their welcome.

"Any luck?" asked Tom, as he ran his boat close to shore.

"Pretty fair. Did you hear from Elmwood?" asked Dick.

"Yes, just got word, and I passed. I'll soon be a Freshman. I wish you fellows were coming along. Come on, get in, and I'll tell you all about it. You've got fish enough."

His chums were glad enough to ride back, and soon, with their fish, they were in the motorboat. While Tom was showing them his letter from the school, Dent managed, by a great effort, to steer properly.

"How soon are you going there?" asked Will.

"In about a week. I hope I make some friends there. I'm going to look up that Senior, Bennington. He told me to."

Talking with his chums of the prospects before him, Tom was soon at his dock again, and this time he locked his boat fast so that Dent could not take it without permission.

"I'm going to let you two fellows run it while I'm at Elmwood," he said to Dick and Will, much to their delight.

The days that followed were busy ones. Mr. and Mrs. Fairfield had much to do, and as for Tom, he had, or imagined he had, so much to take with him, that he thought he would need three trunks at least. But his mother sorted out his clothes, and reduced the number of his other possessions, so that one trunk and a valise sufficed.

In the meanwhile arrangements were made for Tom's father and mother to sail for Australia. Their railroad tickets had been bought, and passage engaged on the steamer Elberon, which was to sail from San Francisco.

"I'm giving you enough money to last you for the term, Tom, I think," said his father. "I want you to have everything you need, but don't be wasteful. I will also leave a further sum in the bank here to your credit, and you will have a check book. But I want you to give me an account of your expenditures."

Tom promised, and felt rather proud to have a bank account, as well as go to a preparatory boarding school. His chums in Briartown envied him more than ever.

At last the day for Tom to start came. His parents were to leave two days later, closing up their house for the fall, for it was early in September.

Good-byes were said, Tom's chums came in numbers to see him off, and with rather a tearful farewell of his father and mother our hero started for school, or rather, college, since Elmwood ranked with upper institutions of learning in conferring degrees.

"Be sure and write," begged Tom's mother.

"I will," he said. "And you write, too."

"Of course," his mother assured him.

The train pulled in, Tom got aboard, and at last he felt that he was really off. He waved his last good-byes, and could not help feeling a little lonesome even though so many pleasures lay before him.

As he took his seat, while his chums cheered and shouted "Rah, Rah, Elmwood!" after him, Tom was aware that a lad across the aisle was regarding him curiously.

This lad was of athletic build. He had red hair, and a pleasant, smiling face.

"Are you going to Elmwood Hall?" he asked Tom.

"Yes," was the answer. "Do you go there?" and then Tom saw that he need not have asked, since he saw the pin of the college on the other's coat.

"I do, Burke's my name—Reddy Burke they all call me. I'm beginning my third year there. Come over and sit with me, and we'll have a talk. Elmwood boys ought to be friendly."

CHAPTER IV

TOM MAKES AN ENEMY

Tom crossed the aisle of the lurching car, and was soon sitting beside the red-haired youth who had made such friendly advances.

"How did you know I was going to Elmwood?" asked our hero, as a sort of opening.

"Easy enough. You've got the air of a fellow going to college for the first time sticking out all over you. Oh, no offense!" exclaimed Reddy Burke as he saw Tom's start. "It's an honor to start at Elmwood Hall. Lots of fellows would like to, but can't. I spotted you for a Freshman right off the bat."

"I suppose I do look a bit green," admitted Tom, with a smile.

"Oh, no more so than usual. Then, too, I heard your friends giving an imitation of the Elmwood yell, and that told me all I wanted to know. I'm glad to meet you. I hope I see more of you when we strike the school. Term opens to-morrow and next day you know, and there'll be no end of fellows there. Opening day generally lasts a week. I thought I'd go down a day early, and get settled in my room."

"That was my idea," confessed Tom.

"Where are you going to put up?"

"I've got a room in Opus Manor. That seemed a nice place, and I picked it out when I came down for the entrance exams.," replied Tom.

"It is nice," admitted Reddy Burke. "It's where all the Freshmen like to get, but usually it's so crowded that you have to go on the waiting list. You're in luck, Fairfield."

"Glad you think so. Where do you room?"

"Oh, I put up with the rest of our crowd at the Ball and Bat. That's our fraternity house you know."

"Yes, I noticed it when I was down before. It's a beaut place, all right."

"Pretty fair. We have some good times there. You must come to some of the blowouts. I'll send you a card when we get settled, and you know the ropes."

"Thanks," replied Tom gratefully. "And now tell me all about Elmwood Hall."

"Oh land! It would take a week!" exclaimed the red-haired athlete. "There's lots to tell about it, but I guess you know the history of it as well as I do, if you've seen a catalog."

"Yes, but I mean tell me something about the fellows, and the professors."

"Well, the professors are no better nor worse than at other colleges, I suppose," spoke Reddy, with something like a sigh. "They all seem to have exaggerated notions about the value of Greek, Latin and mathematics, though I'll be hanged if I like 'em. Baseball and football for mine, though I suppose if I'm ever to become a lawyer, which dad seems to think I'm cut out for, I'll have to buckle down sooner or later, and assimilate some of that dry stuff. It's time I begin, I reckon."

"I should think so—if you're in your Junior year," spoke Tom with a laugh.

"That's right. Oh, I have done some boning, and I haven't cut lectures any more than the rest of the team did. You simply have to cut some if you play all the games, and I didn't miss any contests, you can make up your mind to that. Most all of us at the Ball and Bat play either on the diamond, or gridiron, or row on the crew. I say though, maybe you're that way yourself?" and Reddy looked questioningly at our hero.

"Well," admitted Tom, modestly, "I can row a bit, and I like baseball. I've never played football much. I wasn't quite heavy enough for the team at our Academy."

"You look husky enough," spoke Reddy, casting a critical pair of blue eyes over his seatmate. "You ought to try for the eleven down at Elmwood."

"Maybe I will. Think I'd have a chance?"

"It's too early to say, but have a try, anyhow."

"Are any of the professors very savage?" asked Tom.

"Only so-so. Doctor Pliny Meredith is head master, I suppose you know."

"Yes. How is he?"

"As full of learning as a crab is of meat in the middle of August, but he's not very jolly. Rather stand-offish, and distant, though sometimes he warms up. We call him 'Merry' because he's usually so glum. But he's fair, and he thinks Elmwood Hall the greatest institution ever. To him a fellow's word is as good as his bond. It all goes on the honor system there. No profs. at the exams., you know, and all that. You have to be a gentleman at Elmwood."

"Do the fellows live up to it?" asked Tom.

"Pretty much. There are one or two a little off color, of course. But any fellow who would lie to Merry wouldn't stay long at Elmwood if the fellows got on to it.

"Then, the rest of the profs. are about like the average, except that I don't mind admitting that Burton Skeel is a regular grinder, and as mean as they make 'em. He's the Latin taskmaster and maybe that's why I hate it so."

"Aren't there any jolly professors?" asked Tom, beginning to think that perhaps, after all, he wasn't going to like it at Elmwood as much as he had hoped.

"Oh, bless you, yes!" exclaimed Reddy. "I was almost forgetting Live Wire. That would never do."

"Live Wire? Who's he?"

"Professor Livingston Hammond. He's fat and jolly and he almost makes you like trigonometry, which is saying a lot, and, as for solid geometry, and conic sections, well, if anybody can make them look like the comic sheet of a Sunday newspaper it's the Live Wire. You'll like him; all the fellows do. But he won't stand for any nonsense. You've got to come 'prepared,' or he'll turn you back to make it up after class."

"I like maths.," admitted Tom.

"Then you and the Live Wire will be friends and brothers, I guess," predicted Reddy.

"Tell me something about the fellows," suggested Tom. "I know one Senior, slightly."

"You do? How'd you make his acquaintance?"

"He's Bruce Bennington," replied our hero, as he told of the manner of their first meeting.

"That's odd," commented Reddy. "Bruce is one of the nicest chaps in college. 'Easy Money Bennington' we call him, 'Easy' for short, though. He's a good spender, and his own worst enemy."

"How's that?" asked Tom. "I could see that something was troubling him the day I met him, but he wouldn't say what it was."

"No, that's his way," spoke the red-haired athlete. "I mean that he's impulsive. He'd do anything for a friend, or an enemy too, for that matter, and that often gets him into trouble. He doesn't stop to think, but he's got a host of friends, and everybody likes him, even old Skeel I guess, for I've seen 'em together lots of times."

"I wonder what his special trouble is now?" speculated Tom.

"Give it up. Bruce will never tell until it's settled. He's proud—won't take help from any one if he can help it. So you know him?"

"Well, I hardly can say I know him. He may not want to keep up the acquaintance down here," spoke Tom.

"Oh, yes he will. Bruce isn't that kind. Once he meets you he's always friendly, and, if he takes a notion to you, why you couldn't have a better friend."

Tom was glad to hear this, and he felt a warm spot in his heart for the somewhat unhappy Senior. He resolved to find out his trouble, if he could, and help him if it were possible.

"Of course there are some mean and undesirable chaps at Elmwood," admitted Reddy. "Just as there are anywhere, I guess, only I wouldn't want to name any of 'em. You'll find out who they are, soon enough. But you just play straight and they'll soon let you alone. They may try to pick a quarrel, and there are a few who are always trying to get up a mill. Do you fight?"

"I box a little," admitted Tom.

"Good, then you can take care of yourself if it comes to a scrap, I suppose. But don't get into a fight if you can help it. Not that I mean to run away, but it's against the rules to fight, and you don't want to be suspended, though there are more or less mills pulled off every term."

"I'll fight if I have to; not otherwise," spoke Tom, quietly.

"Good. Say, you'll think I'm trying to put it all over you, and do the big brother act with such advice; won't you?"

"Not a bit of it," replied Tom, stoutly. "I'm glad to have you give me points."

"All right then. I guess you'll do. We've got one funny character at the school—Demosthenes Miller."

"A student?"

"Land no. He's our educated janitor. He's always around with a copy of the classics, or some book on maths., and if he sees you getting at all friendly he'll ask you to help him translate a passage, or work out a problem. He says he might as well be getting an education on the side as long as he's at college. He's good fun, but rather tiresome at times. Demy, we call him."

"He must be odd," agreed Tom.

"There! I guess I've told you all I know," spoke Reddy, with a laugh. "The rest you'll find out after you've been at the school a few days. Now tell me something about yourself."

Which Tom did, mentioning about his father and mother going to Australia.

"That's a trip I'd like to take," said Reddy. "Cracky, what sport! I love travel."

The lads talked on various topics as the train sped along. They were nearing Elmwood Hall, which was located in the town of the same name, on the Ware river. Several other lads, whom Reddy pointed out to Tom as old or new students, had meanwhile boarded the train. A number greeted Tom's seatmate as an old friend and our hero was introduced to them. They greeted him nicely enough, but talked to Reddy.

Soon the latter was deep in conversation about the chances for a good football season, and Tom did not like to break in, but listened with all his might.

"Here we are, Fairfield," said Reddy Burke, at length. "Get your grip, and I'll show you the way to the Hall. Oh, I forgot, you've been here before, though."

"Yes, I can find my way up well enough," spoke Tom. "Don't let me hold you back."

"All right then. I'll see you later. There's Hen Mattock up ahead. He was football captain last year. I want to talk to him, so I'll just run on. See you again!" and with that Reddy rushed off, to clap on the shoulder a tall, well-built lad, who looked every inch an athlete. Tom gathered up his belongings, gave his trunk check to an expressman, and headed for Opus Manor.

This residence, or dormitory, was one of the school buildings, located not far away from the main hall and was "within bounds," so that the Freshmen, did they wish to spend an evening in town, had to get permission, or else "run the guard," a proceeding fraught with some danger, carrying with detection a penalty more or less severe. It was the aim of the school proctor, Mr. Frederick Porter, to thus keep watch and ward over the first year students.

The others were allowed more liberty, or at least they took it, for many of them lived in fraternity houses, and some Seniors boarded in private families in town. Most of the Seniors, however, dwelt in a house near the Hall. It was called Elmwood Castle, and Tom looked longingly at it as he passed on his way to his own more humble, and less distinctive, dormitory.

As Tom was ascending the steps, intending to report to the monitor in charge, and also seek out the matron, he became aware of a student standing on the topmost platform, looking down at him. Beside him was another lad, and, as our hero came up, one shoved the other against Tom, jostling him severely.

Instantly Tom flared up. He could see that it was done intentionally. His face flushed.

"What do you mean?" he asked quickly.

"Whatever you like to think," was the reply of the student whom Tom had first noticed.

"Well, I think I don't like it," retorted Tom quickly.

"You'll have to get used to it then; won't he, Nick?" and the lad who had done the shoving appealed to his companion, with a sneering laugh.

"That's what he will, Sam."

"I won't then!" exclaimed Tom, "and the sooner you realize that the better."

"Oh ho! So that's the kind of talk, eh?" sneered the one called Sam. "What's your name, Fresh?"

"Fairfield—Tom Fairfield—Fresh!" retorted Tom, for he could see by the other's cap that he, too, was a first year lad.

"Well mine's Heller—Sam Heller, Capital 'S' and capital 'H,' and don't forget it. This must be the fellow who's got my room, Nick," he added.

"Probably," replied Sam Heller's crony, who was Nick Johnson. "Yes, that was the name the monitor mentioned, come to think of it."

"How have I your room?" asked Tom.

"Because you have. I had the room last year, and I told 'em to save it for me this term. But you came along and snatched it up, so—"

"I took it because it was assigned to me," spoke Tom, and from the other's talk he understood that the lad was a Freshman who had not passed, and who, in consequence, was obliged to spend another year in the same grade. Perhaps this made him bitter.

"Well, you've got my room," grumbled Sam, "and I'm going to get square with somebody."

"You can get square with me, if you like," said Tom quietly, "though I told you I had nothing to do with it. One thing, though, if you do any more shoving I'll shove back, and it won't be a gentle shove, either."

"Is that a threat?" growled Sam.

"You can take it so if you like."

"I will, and if you don't look out—"

What Sam was going to say he did not finish, for, at that moment, the monitor in charge of Opus Manor came to the door, and the two who had sought to pick a quarrel with Tom slouched off across the campus.

"New student here?" asked the monitor, who did not seem to remember Tom.

"Yes. I'm Fairfield."

"Oh yes, I recall you now. Come, and I'll introduce you to my wife. She's matron here. Blackford is my name."

"I remember it," spoke Tom, who had met the monitor when down for his examinations.

As the two were about to enter the building Tom saw his new friend, Reddy Burke, hurrying along, beckoning to him to wait.

He halted a moment, and the Junior ran up the steps.

"I just saw you talking here to a couple of students," began the athlete, "and as I passed them just now I heard Sam Heller say he was going to get even with you. What happened?"

Tom told him and Reddy whistled.

"Why, what's up?" asked our hero.

"Nothing, if you don't mind it, only you've made an enemy right off the bat. That Heller is one of the few undesirables here. His crony, Nick Johnson, is another. Heller is down on you all right, though it isn't your fault."

"I don't mind in the least," spoke Tom.

"He's one of the scrappers," went on Reddy. "Look out!"

"I can take care of myself," replied Tom. "Thanks, just the same," and, as he followed Monitor Blackford into the dormitory, he realized that he had made an enemy and a friend in the same day.

CHAPTER V

TOM FINDS A CHUM

"This is the room assigned to you," said the monitor, pausing in a long corridor, after he had introduced Tom to Mrs. Blackford. "It is one of the best in the Manor, though I don't quite understand why you picked out a double apartment."

"Is it a double one?" asked Tom in some surprise. "I did not know it. As I was requested in the circular I received, I indicated the section of the building where I would like to be, and this room was assigned to me. I supposed it was a single one."

"No, it is intended for two students, and I suppose it was assigned to you by mistake. I'm sorry, as it is too late to change now, since all the reservations are taken, and—"

"Oh, I don't want to change!" exclaimed Tom quickly, as he entered the apartment shown him by the monitor. He saw that there were two beds in it, and that it was large and airy. "I'll keep this," our hero added. "It's fine."

"Have you a chum who might like to share it with you?" asked Blackford. "The expense may—"

"Oh, I don't mind that part of it," said Tom. "My father knew how much it was to cost, and he did not object. I haven't a friend yet—that is, a Freshman friend—but I may find one."

"There is one, a Sam Heller, who had this room last term," went on the monitor. "He would doubtless be very glad to come in with you."

"I'm afraid not," replied Tom with a smile. "He and I had a little difference of opinion just now, and—"

"Very well," interrupted Mr. Blackford. "You needn't explain. Suit yourself about the room. It is yours for the term." He knew better than to enter into a talk about the disagreements of the students. There were other troubles to occupy him.

Left to himself, Tom sat down and looked about the room that was to be his for the Freshman year. It had a good view of the campus and buildings, and he liked it very much.

"Though I should be glad if I had a good chum to come in with me," reflected the new student. "I may get in with somebody, though. It's rather lonesome to have two beds in one room, but I can sleep half the night in one, and half the night in the other I suppose," he ended, with a smile.

Tom was unpacking his belongings from his valise when the expressman arrived with his trunk, and a little later the matron knocked at the door to ask if our hero found himself at home.

"Yes, thank you," replied Tom, accepting the clean towels she brought. He had begun to hang up his clothes.

"I do hope you get a nice young man in with you," suggested Mrs. Blackford. "One who won't be cutting up, and doing all sorts of mischievous pranks."

Tom proceeded with getting his room to rights as she left him, and a little later, finding that it wanted an hour yet to twelve o'clock, our hero strolled out on the campus.

He looked about for a sight of Sam Heller, or his crony, Johnson, who, it appeared later, had passed his examinations, and was a Sophomore, while Sam had to remain a Freshman, much to his disgust. But the two, whom Tom had come to feel were his enemies, were not in sight. Nor was Reddy Burke, and, though Tom strolled over past Elmwood Castle, he did not get a sight of Bruce Bennington.

Tom strolled about until lunch, and the mid-day meal was not a very jolly affair. About twenty Freshmen, who had come a day before the term formally opened, were at the tables and they were all rather miserable, like fishes out of water, as Tom reflected. Still our hero talked with them, experiences were exchanged, and the ice was broken.

"But I don't exactly cotton to any of them enough to have one for a roommate," reflected Tom.

That afternoon, having formally registered, and being told about the hours for chapel, and his lecture and recitation periods, Tom wrote a long letter to his father and mother.

He was coming back, from having posted it, when he noticed, standing on the steps of Opus Manor, a solitary figure.

"I hope that isn't Sam Heller, waiting to renew the quarrel with me," reflected Tom, as he drew nearer. "Still, if it is, I'll meet him half way, though I don't want to get into a fight my first day here."

But he was soon made aware that it was not the bully who stood on the steps. It was a lad about his own age, a tall, straight youth, with a pleasant smiling face, and merry brown eyes. No, I am just a trifle wrong about that face. It was naturally a jolly one, but just now it bore a puzzled and unhappy look.

"Hello," said Tom pleasantly, as he mounted the steps, and was about to pass in.

"Hello!" greeted the other. "Do you room here?"

"Yes. This is my first day."

"Say, you're in luck. It's my first day too. I'm a stranger in a strange land, and I'm stuck."

"What's the matter?" asked Tom.

"Well, very foolishly, I delayed settling about my room until I got here. I thought there'd be plenty of places, and, when I did arrive I found that Opus Manor was the only desirable place for us Freshmen. Up I steps, as bold as brass, and asks for a room and bath. 'Nothing doing,' answers the worthy monitor, or words to that effect. Consequently, behold yours truly without a place to sleep, unless he goes into town to a common boarding house. And I did want to get in with the Freshmen! It's tough luck!"

Tom was doing some rapid thinking.

"I don't suppose you know of a good place in town; do you?" went on the other. "My name is Fitch—Jack Fitch. I'm from New York city."

"Mine's Tom Fairfield, from Briartown," said our hero.

"Well, Tom Fairfield, have you been here long enough to recommend a place to room, where I can also get the eats; especially the eats, for I'm a good feeder. Know of a likely place?"

Tom's mind was made up.

"Yes, there's a place here," he said.

"Here? Are you stringing me? They told me every room was taken."

"So it is, but I have a large double one, and I was looking for a chum. So—"

"You don't mean you'll take me in?" cried Jack. "Oh, end the suspense! Fireman save my child! Don't torture me!" and he gave a good imitation of a woe-begone actor.

"I'll be glad to have you," said Tom, who had taken a sudden liking to Jack. "That is, if you'd really like to come. You might look at the room."

"Say no more! Come? Of course I'll come! Will a duck swim? But I say, you know, you don't know much about me."

"I'll take a chance—if you will," said Tom, laughing.

"All right. Then we'll call it square. Lead on and I'll follow. To think that, after all, I'm going to get in Opus Manor! It's great, Fairfield!"

"Call me Tom, if you like."

"I like. I'm Jack to you, from now on. Shake!" and he caught Tom's hand in a firm clasp. The two looked into each other's eyes, and what they read satisfied them. They were chums from then on.

"I'll take you to my room—our room," Tom corrected himself. "It's a fine one!"

"I'm sure it must be. But do you reckon the Lord and Lady of this castle will allow me to share it with you?"

"Yes. In fact Mrs. Blackford spoke of me getting some one in with me. So that will be all right."

"Great! Do you mind if I do a little dance? Just a few steps to show my joy?" asked Jack, and Tom perceived at once that his new friend was a jolly lad.

"Not at all," Tom answered, and Jack gravely did a hop skip and jump on the top platform of the steps.

As he finished there came a laugh from a couple of lads passing.

"Look at the ballet lady!" mocked a voice, and Tom saw Sam Heller and Nick Johnson approaching.

"Did you like it?" asked Jack, coolly. He was not to be easily disconcerted.

"Oh, it was great!" declared Sam with a sneer. "We'll have you in the Patchwork Club if you keep on."

There was no mistaking the sneering tone of his voice, and Jack flushed.

"Friends of yours?" he asked Tom.

"Just the reverse. But don't bother with them now. We can attend to them later—if we have to."

"And I think I shall have to," said Jack quietly, as he looked Sam full in the face. "I don't mind fun, but I like it to come from my friends. Lead on, Tom, and, as you say, we'll attend to those two later."

He followed Tom, and, as they disappeared into Opus Manor there floated to them the mocking laughs of the two cronies.

CHAPTER VI

AN ANGRY PROFESSOR

"Tom, did you ever balance a water pitcher on your nose? I mean full of water. The pitcher full, that is to say, not the nose."

"Never, and I'm not going to begin now."

"Well, I am. Watch me. I used to be pretty good at juggling."

"Say, you want to be careful."

"Oh, I will be. I've never done it, but there must always be a first time. And, though balancing water pitchers may not be an accomplishment taught in all schools, still there may come a time when the knowledge of how to juggle one will come in handy. Here goes."

Tom and Jack were in their room—the room our hero had decided to share with his new chum. The matron and monitor had been interviewed, and Mrs. Blackford was very glad, she said, to know that Tom was to have a companion.

"And such a nice, quiet-appearing lad as he is, too," she confided to her husband. Alas, she did not know Jack Fitch!

"The other one seems very quiet, also," said Mr. Blackford. "I wish all the students were like those two."

But if he and his wife could have looked into the chums' room at that moment, perhaps they would not have held to that opinion.

For Jack had taken the large water pitcher, and was preparing to balance it on his nose, while Tom, rather fearing how the experiment would terminate, had gotten safely out of the way in case of an accident.

"I wouldn't do it, if I were you," spoke Tom, though he could not help laughing at his chum's odd notion.

"Why not?" demanded Jack.

"Well—— Oh, because it might fall."

"No reason at all, Tom. If would-be jugglers hesitated on that account there'd be no experts. Give me a hand until I get it up on my nose; will you?"

"I'd rather not."

"Why?"

"I'm afraid it will fall."

"Oh, pshaw! Why fear? Never mind. I'll balance it on my chin instead of my nose. On second thought it's a little too heavy for the nose act, and my nose is like a bear's—it's tender. Watch me!"

Jack carefully lifted the pitcher of water, and managed to get it on his chin. He steadied it with his two hands, bending his head back, and then, when he thought he had it where he wanted it, he lowered his palms, and the pitcher—for an instant—was balanced on his chin.

"Look!" he called to Tom, not taking his eyes from the vessel of water. "Talk about jugglers! Some class to me; eh, Tom?"

"Yes, I guess so."

"Now bring me a chair," requested Jack. "I'm going to do it standing on a chair."

"You'll never do it!" predicted Tom.

"Yes, I will. I'll get the chair myself, then."

This was his undoing. As long as he remained in one spot, with his head carefully held still, the pitcher did not tilt enough to upset. But, as soon as Jack moved, there was an accident.

"Look out!" yelled Tom, but his warning came too late.

Jack made a wild grab for the slipping vessel, but his hands did not grasp it in time. A moment later there was a heavy crash, pieces of china flew about the room, and a shower of water drenched the chums.

For a moment there was a grim silence. Then Jack said:

"Well, I'll be jiggered!"

"You certainly ought to be!" and Tom laughed in spite of himself, for his new chum was much wetter than he.

The sound of rapidly approaching footsteps was heard.

"Oh pip!" whispered the luckless juggler.

"What is the matter? Has anything happened?" demanded the voice of Matron Blackford, in the corridor.

"Well—er—yes—we have had a slight—er—happening," replied Tom, grabbing the clean towels, and proceeding to mop up the water from the carpet.

"Oh, is anyone hurt? May I come in?"

"Come!" called Jack, following his chum's example, and the matron entered.

"What happened?" she asked, as she saw the water, the drenched boys, and the pieces of the broken pitcher.

"It—it sort of—fell," replied Jack calmly, mopping away at the carpet.

"And broke," added Tom. "We're sorry——"

"And the water all spilled out," needlessly interrupted Jack. "We are very sorry for that, too."

"Oh you boys!" exclaimed the matron, raising her hands in despair. "I was afraid something would happen. What were you doing?"

"I was reciting my lesson in juggling," replied Jack gravely. "And the pitcher slipped. I'll pay for it."

"Oh, no, as long as you were at your lessons when it happened, it was an accident, and you needn't pay," said the matron, but, later, Jack insisted, and then the story came out.

"I'll bring you some clean towels," said Mrs. Blackford. "Luckily there is a wooden ceiling below, or the plaster would have fallen, if there had been any," and she hurried away.

Tom's first day at Elmwood Hall ended quietly enough, as did Jack's, at dinner in the big Freshman class dining room, and the two went to bed early, as they were rather tired. There was very little excitement in the school that night. A few of the older students sang some choruses on the campus, but the real life of the institution had not yet begun.

The next day was full of activity. Students—old and new—arrived by the score, and the professors, the matrons, the monitors, the proctor, and Doctor Meredith himself, had their hands full. Opus Manor filled with a laughing, chattering crowd, and Tom was glad he had selected his room in advance, as there were many disappointed boys, when they found they could not get the apartments they wanted.

"I struck it right!" declared Jack.

"And so did I!" added Tom, for he liked his new chum more and more. They made the acquaintance of several lads. On one side of them roomed Bert Wilson, to whom Tom and Jack at once took a liking, and on the other side was George Abbot, a rather lonely little chap.

"I'm sure we're going to like it here," declared Jack, after their first lecture, when both he and Tom found that they were well up in the subject presented.

"Sure," assented Tom.

"It's a jolly place, all right," declared Bert. "I wonder if there'll be any hazing?"

"Of course," declared Jack. "I don't mind, though."

"Nor I," said Tom.

Several days passed, and nearly all the students, save a few Seniors, had arrived. Bruce Bennington was among the missing, and Tom found himself wondering if he would come back.

"Maybe his trouble will keep him out of college," thought our hero, and he felt some regret, for he had formed a liking for the lad, though he had met him but once.

"Come on down to the river," proposed Tom one day, after the last lecture for himself and his chum. "I'm just aching to get into a boat, and I understand there are some on the Ware river that a fellow can hire. I wish I had my motorboat here."

"Why don't you send for it?"

"Guess I will. Say, don't you think the Latin is pretty stiff here?"

"A bit. But old Skeel makes it so. He's fierce. I guess Reddy Burke was right about what he said of him."

"Sure he was. But never mind. Maybe it'll be easier when we've been here a few weeks. Here's a short cut to the river," suggested Tom, as they came to the rear of a fine residence. "Let's take it."

"Looks as if we'd have to cross private grounds. One of the profs. lives here, I understand."

"What of it?" asked our hero. "He won't mind, I guess. I like to take cut-offs when I can."

"Go ahead. I'm with you," answered Jack.

The two cut across a lawn in the rear of the house, for they could see the glittering river just beyond a fringe of trees, and they were glad of the by-path, as they had gone a longer and more roundabout way several times.

Tom was in the lead, and he had just passed a summer house, vine-encumbered, on the rear lawn, when an angry voice hailed him.

"Where are you going?" was demanded.

"To the river," replied Tom.

"Who told you to go this way?"

"No one."

As Tom answered he saw a man come from the summer house, a man he at once recognized as Professor Burton Skeel, the grim Latin instructor.

"Well, you boys can just go back the way you came," went on the angry professor. "These are my private grounds, and I allow no students to trespass. If I find you doing it again I shall take sterner measures. Go back the way you came, and don't come here again. Ah, I see that you are Elmwood students," the professor went on. "That makes it all the worse. You should have known that I permit no trespassing, nor trifling. Be off!"

He fairly yelled the last words at the chums, who, though abashed, were not much alarmed by the angry instructor.

As they turned to retrace their steps Tom saw another figure in the summer house. He had a glimpse of the face, and it was that of Bruce Bennington. The Senior had been in close conversation with the angry professor.

"He looks sad," mused Tom, referring to Bruce. "I guess his trouble isn't over yet. I wonder if that glum professor can have anything to do with it?"

CHAPTER VII

BRUCE IS WORRIED

"Nice, pleasant sort of a chap for a professor—not!" exclaimed Jack, as he and Tom went a more roundabout, and public, way to the river.

"He certainly is grouchy," agreed our hero. "Who'd think he'd rile up just because we cut through his back yard? He may take it out of us in class."

"Shouldn't wonder. His kind usually does."

"Did you see who was with him?" asked Tom.

"I saw a fellow, but no one I knew."

"That was Bruce Bennington, the Senior I was telling you about."

"The one you said had some trouble?"

"Yes, and to judge by his looks he has it yet. I wonder what he was doing with old Skeel?"

"Maybe explaining why he hadn't been to lectures before this."

"No, I understand the Senior class doesn't have to report as punctually as we poor dubs of Freshmen. It must be something else."

"Well, we have our own troubles, Tom. Don't go to looking for those of other fellows."

"I won't, Jack, only I'd like to help Bennington if I could."

"So would I. Look, there are some boats we might hire," and Tom pointed to a small structure on the edge of the river, where several boats were tied. A number of students from Elmwood Hall were gathered about, and some were out in the rowing craft.

Tom and Jack learned that the man in charge kept boats for hire, and the two chums were soon out in one, pulling up the river so, as Tom explained, they would have it easier coming back with the current.

"There goes the Senior shell!" exclaimed Jack, as from the college boathouse the long, slender craft was rowed out, looking not unlike some big bug, with long, slender legs. "They're practicing for the race, I guess."

"I wish I was with them," remarked Tom. "I'm going to try for the Freshman crew."

"And I'm with you."

The two rowed on, and soon found a quiet, shady nook, where the trees overhung the river. There they tied their boat, and talked in the shadows.

Coming back they again saw the Senior shell, the lads in it rowing more slowly, for they were tired after their practice sprint. Turning in their hired boat, Tom and Jack went to the college crew's headquarters, and there Tom, on making cautious inquiries, learned to his regret that there would be no Freshman crew organized that fall.

"You see," explained Reddy Burke to the two lads, who were much interested in water sports, "our rowing season is in the spring. This is only a little supplementary race the head crew is going to row with Burkhardt college, which is five miles down stream. We beat them in the spring, but they asked for another meet, and we gave it to them.

"But rowing is practically over for this year, so I guess there's no chance for you to get in a shell. Try in the spring, if you want to."

"We will," decided Tom.

"Meanwhile you'd better be thinking of football," advised Reddy. "Candidates for the team as well as for the class elevens will soon be called for."

"That hits us!" exclaimed Jack. "I'm going to train hard. Do you think our crew will win."

"Sure," declared Reddy, and I might add here that when the auxiliary race was rowed, two weeks later, Elmwood did win easily over her rival.

"Bennington is here," remarked Tom, as with Jack he walked toward the campus with Reddy.

"Is that so? It's about time he blew in. Where did you see him?"

Tom explained, telling of the peremptory manner in which Professor Skeel had ordered them from his lawn.

"Oh, you mustn't mind that," advised Reddy. "He certainly is getting worse every term. I don't see why Dr. Meredith keeps him. He's the worst one of the faculty, and if he doesn't look out he'll get what's coming to him."

"Well, what shall we do this evening?" asked Jack, as he and his chum were in their room after supper. "I've done with my boning."

"So have I. What do you say to a lark? Let's run the guard and go to town."

"I'm with you. Let's get some of the other fellows," proposed Jack. "Bert Wilson will come, and so will George Abbot, I guess, if he can stop asking questions long enough."

"Sure we'll go," declared Bert, when the chums made the proposal to him.

"But what will we do when we get there?" George wanted to know.

"Oh. Why, we'll stand on our heads!" exclaimed Tom with a laugh.

"All of us?" demanded the inquisitive lad.

"No, only you," retorted Jack. "For cats' sake, cut out some of those questions; will you? We'll call you Interrogation Mark if you don't look out, only it's too much of a mouthful to speak in a hurry. Cut along now, before we're caught."

It was dark enough to elude a possible spying monitor, or one of the proctor's emissaries, and soon the four lads were on their way to town. They went to a moving picture show, enjoying it greatly.

"Now if we can get in without being seen, we'll be all right," remarked Tom, when they had neared the college on the return trip.

"Pshaw, I shouldn't much mind getting caught," declared Jack. "It would be fun."

"Doing double boning, or being kept in bounds for a week wouldn't though," declared Tom with conviction. "I vote we don't get caught, if we can help it."

"Maybe we can't," suggested Bert.

"Why not?" George wanted to know.

"Oh, ask us something easier," laughed Tom. "Come on now, and don't make too much noise."

They were about to cross the campus, and make for their dormitory, when there was a movement behind a clump of shrubbery, and a figure was seen to emerge.

"There's some one!" whispered Bert.

"Caught!" murmured Tom.

"I wonder who it is?" came from George.

"It's Bruce Bennington, the Senior," came from Tom. "We are safe."

"You won't be if you continue on this way," came grimly from Bruce. "One of the proctor's scouts is out to-night, just laying for innocent Freshies. You'd better cut around the side, and go in the back basement door. It's generally open, or if it isn't I've got a key that will do the trick."

"You know the ropes," laughed Tom.

"I ought to. I was a Freshman once. Come on, I'll show you the way, but don't work the trick too often."

Bruce walked up to Tom, and remarked:

"Oh, it's you, is it, Fairfield. Glad to see you again. I didn't recognize you in the darkness. I just got in to-day."

"Yes, I saw you," remarked our hero as he introduced his chums.

Bruce continued to walk on beside Tom, the others following. The Senior led the way along a little-used path, well screened by trees from spying eyes.

"Won't you get caught yourself?" Tom wanted to know.

"No, we lordly Seniors are allowed a few more privileges than you luckless squabs. Though I shouldn't much mind if I was nabbed. It would be like old times," and Tom detected a sigh in the words. Clearly Bruce was still worrying.

"I saw you in Professor Skeel's summer house this afternoon," went on Tom.

"Oh, so you were the lads he warned away! Yes, Skeel is a—well I guess I'd better not say anything," spoke Bruce quickly. "It might not be altogether healthy."

"For you?" asked Tom.

"Yes. I'm under some obligations to him, and—well, I don't like to talk about it," he finished.

"Then you haven't gotten over your trouble?" asked Tom sympathetically.

"No, it's worse than ever. Oh, hang it all, what a chump I've been!" exclaimed Bruce. "This thing is worrying the life out of me!"

"Why can't some of your friends help you?" asked Tom. "If I could——"

"No, thank you, Fairfield, no one can do anything but myself, and I can't, just now. It may come out all right in the end. Don't say anything about it. Here we are. Now to see if the door's open."

Letting Bruce lead the way, the other lads cautiously followed. They saw him about to try the knob of the basement portal, when suddenly Tom became aware of a light flickering through a side window.

"Hist!" he signalled to Bruce. "Someone's coming!"

"All right. You fellows lay low, and I'll take a look," volunteered their guide. "I don't mind being caught."

"He's got nerve," said Jack, admiringly, as he and his chums crouched down in the darkness.

Tom and the others saw Bruce boldly look in the window through which the light shone.

CHAPTER VIII

THE CALL OF THE PIGSKIN

"Maybe it's Professor Skeel," whispered George, apprehensively.

"Or Merry himself," added Jack.

"Nonsense!" replied Tom. "Neither of them would be in our dormitory at this hour."

"Unless they got wise to the fact that we went out, and they're laying to catch us when we come in," declared Bert. "If I'm nabbed I hope my dad doesn't hear of it."

"Come on, fellows," came in a shrill whisper from Bruce. "It's only Demy, our studious janitor. He's boning over some book, and if you help him with his conjugation, or demonstrate a geometric proposition for him, he'll let you burn the school down and say nothing about it. Come on; it's all right."

They entered through the door, which was not locked, so that Bruce did not have to use his key, and at their advance, into what was a sort of storeroom of the basement, the studious janitor looked up from a book he was reading.

"Well, well!" he exclaimed. "Is this—ahem! young gentleman, I hardly know what——"

"It's all right, Demy," interrupted Bruce with a laugh. "I brought 'em in. They want to help you do a little—let's see what you're at, anyhow?" and he looked at the book.

"It's Horace," said the janitor. "I want to read some of his odes in the original, but the translating is very hard, to say the least. Still, I am determined to get an education while I have the chance."

"Good for you!" exclaimed the Senior. "I'll help you, Demy. Horace is pie for me. You fellows cut along to your rooms," he added, significantly. "You haven't seen them, have you, Demy?"

"No, Mr. Bennington, not if you don't wish me to," and the janitor, with a grateful look at the Senior, prepared to listen to the Latin, while Tom and his chums, grateful for the aid given them, hurried up the stairs to their apartments.

"That was fine of him, wasn't it?" remarked Jack, as good-nights were being whispered.

"It sure was," declared Tom, wishing more than ever that he could help the unhappy Senior.

"I wonder why the janitor wants to know Latin?" came from the human question mark.

"Oh, answer that in your dreams," advised Tom.

From the fact that no mention was made of their little night excursion, Tom and the others concluded that the studious janitor had kept his pact with Bruce. The latter told Tom afterward that he was kept busy giving Latin instruction until nearly midnight.

"It was good of you," said our hero.

"Oh, pshaw! I'm glad I can do somebody good," was the rejoinder. That was Bruce Bennington's way. As Reddy had said, the Senior was his own worst enemy.

"Hear the news?" burst out Jack, as he entered the room where Tom was studying, a few afternoons later.

"No, what news?"

"Call for Freshmen and regular football candidates is posted. Practice begins to-morrow. Let's get out our suits."

"Fine!" cried Tom, tossing his book on the table, and scurrying for his trunk where he had packed away his moleskin trousers and canvas jacket. Jack soon had his out, looking for possible rents and ripped seams.

"I've got to do some mending—worse luck!" exclaimed Tom, as he saw a big hole in his trousers.

"Can you sew?" asked Jack.

"Oh, so-so," laughed Tom. "I can make a stab at it, anyhow," and he proceeded to close up the rent by the simple process of gathering the edges together like the mouth of a bag, and winding string around them. "There! I guess that'll do," he added.

It was a clear, crisp day, and "the call of the pigskin" had been heard all through the college. Several score of lads, in more or less disreputable suits, that had seen lots of service, assembled on the gridiron under the watchful eyes of the coaches.

"I hope I make the regular eleven," said Tom, as he sent a beautiful spiral kick to Jack.

"So do I," was the reply. "But I hear there are lots of candidates for it, and almost a whole team was left over from last season, so there won't be much chance for us."

The practice was more or less ragged, and, in fact it was only designed to let the coaches see how the new lads "sized-up." Several elevens were tentatively formed, and taken to different parts of the field to play against each other.

Tom worked hard, and he was glad to note that one of the older players had regarded him with what our hero thought were favorable eyes. Jack was also doing well.

This practice was kept up for several days, and about a week later Reddy Burke, meeting Tom, exclaimed:

"Say, you fellows are in luck!"

"How so?" asked Jack, who was with his chum.

"You've made the eleven, I hear. You'll probably get notice to-day."

"The regular?" cried Tom in delight.

"Hardly! There's only one new fellow going on that, I understand, though you might fill in as subs. But you're both going to play on the first Freshman eleven."

"The Freshman team," spoke Jack, somewhat disappointedly.

"Say, what do you want?" asked Tom. "I think it's fine. Of course I wish it was the regular, but maybe next year——"

"That's the way to talk," declared Reddy, who was on the leading team himself. "But I tell you that you're in luck to make the Freshman team. There are no end of candidates, but you two seemed to hit the mark."

Tom rejoiced exceedingly, and when he received his formal notice, as did Jack, our hero at once wrote to his parents, who were soon to reach Australia. Tom had had several letters from them since leaving home, but had yet to hear of their safe arrival. He sent the letter to Sydney, in care of his father's lawyer.

There were busy days for our hero and his chums now. With lectures to attend, studying to do, and football practice, their time was pretty well occupied. Bert Wilson had made the Freshman eleven, and the three chums played well together.

Tom had not seen much of Bruce Bennington since the night the Senior aided the first year lads, for Bruce was busy too, as he was on the 'varsity.

Tom found that football, as played at Elmwood, was very different from the Academy games, but he was made of tough material, and he soon worked well into his place as right half-back, while Jack was left tackle. Several scrub games had been played, and the Freshman coaches seemed satisfied with the work of their charges.

"Hurray!" yelled Tom, running up to Jack one afternoon, as his chum was strolling across the campus. "Yell, old man!"

"What for?"

"We play our first regular game Saturday against Holwell college. They've got a strong team, but we're going to win! I'm going to make a touchdown!"

"Good! Oh, say, it's great here!" and in the excess of their good spirits Tom and Jack fell to pummelling each other in hearty fashion.

CHAPTER IX

TOM'S TOUCHDOWN

"Come on now, boys, line up!"

It was the call of Coach Jackson for the final practice of the Freshmen eleven before their first big game. The regulars were to play against the scrub, and, as some of the positions were yet in doubt, there were some anxious hearts. For not a substitute but wanted to fill in on the regular eleven.

Tom and Jack, because of the good showing they had made, were assured of places, but Sam Heller, who, to do him credit, was a fairly good player, was not so certain. It lay between him and Bert Wilson, as to who would be quarter-back.

"But if I had my rights, and if that Fairfield chap hadn't come butting in," declared Sam to his crony, Nick, "I would be sure of my place."

"That's right," agreed Nick. "We'll have to get up something on Fairfield, and make him quit Elmwood."

"I wish I could. Say, the Sophs haven't done any hazing this term yet; have they?"

"No, but they will."

"I suppose so. Well, just have 'em let me down easy; will you? I'm a Soph myself, by rights, if old Hammond hadn't marked me low in maths. But have the Sophs give it to Fairfield and his chum good and proper; will you?"

"Sure I will. We're going to do some hazing after the football game. We thought we'd put it off until then."

"All right, only do Tom Fairfield up if you can."

"I will. I don't like him any more than you do. He's got too many airs to suit me—he and that Jack Fitch."

"Line up! Line up!" called the coach, and the practice began. Sam Heller was called on to take his place in the scrub, which he did with no good grace, casting envious eyes at Bert Wilson, and with a feeling of bitterness in his heart toward Tom. And with no good cause, for Tom had done nothing to Sam.

"Now, boys, play your heads off!" ordered the coach. "I want to see what sort of stuff you're made of. The best players will go against Holwell to-morrow."

Then the scrub game began, with the Freshmen players doing their best to shove back their opponents, and the latter equally determined to make as good a showing as possible. Back and forth the battle of the gridiron waged, with Tom jumping into every play, looking for openings where he might wriggle through with the ball, or help the man who had it to gain a yard or two.

"Touchdown! Touchdown!" yelled the members of the first eleven, as they got the ball well down toward the scrub goal. "Make it a touchdown!"

It would have been, but for the fact that Bert Wilson fumbled the ball in passing it back from centre. A scrub player broke through, grabbed the pigskin, and was off down the field like a shot.

"Get him, boys!" cried Morse Denton, the Freshman captain, and Jack Fitch, who was as fleet as some ends, was after the fleeing youth. He caught him in time to prevent a score being made, but the coach shook his head at the next line up.

"Heller, you go in at quarter to replace Wilson," he said. "I am sorry," the arbiter added, at the look of gloom on the face of Tom's chum, "but fumbles are costly. I can't afford to take any chances."

Bert said nothing, but he knew that he was not altogether at fault, for the centre had not passed the ball accurately. Sam Heller, with a triumphant smile at Tom, went to quarter, and the game proceeded. But it was noticed that Sam, who was giving signals, and deciding on most of the plays, did not give Tom as many chances as when Bert had been in place behind the centre.

"You want to look out for Sam in the game to-morrow," said Jack to Tom that night, when, after gruelling practice, the regular Freshmen had shoved the scrub all over the field.

"Why so?"

"Because I think he has it in for you. He'll spoil your plays if he can, and he won't give you a chance. Look out for him."

"I will. But at the same time I don't believe he'd do anything to spoil the chance of the team winning."

"I wouldn't trust him. At the same time he may do nothing worse than not give you a chance. It's going to be a big game, I hear, and the fellow who makes good will be in line for the 'varsity next season."

"I'll watch out. Now let's do something. Come on in Bert's room. He feels bad about not playing to-morrow."

"I know. But it's forbidden to visit in other fellows' rooms after hours."

"Oh, what of it?" asked Tom, who liked to take chances. "We've got to do something. It isn't so late, and there are no lectures to-morrow."

"All right, go ahead. I'm with you. But I hope we don't get caught. It might mean being ruled out of the game to-morrow."

Bert was grateful for the sympathy of his chums, and soon felt in better humor. Jack offered to repeat his water pitcher juggling act, and was only prevented by force on the part of Tom. There was a merry scuffle, and George Abbot came in to see what was going on, at the same time bringing warning that a sub-monitor had been patroling the corridors.

"Then we've got to be quiet," declared Tom. "Cut out your juggling, Jack."

The four chums talked for an hour or more, and then the three, who were out of their rooms, taking a cautious survey of the hall, prepared to go to bed, ready for the big game on the morrow. Jack and Tom just escaped being caught as they slipped into their apartment, but, as Tom remarked, "A miss was as good as a mile."

Then came the day of the great game.

"Line up! Line up!"

"Over here, Elmwood!"

"This way, Holwell!"

"Rah! Rah! Rah!"

"Toot! Toot! Toot!"

These were only some of the cries that burst forth from hundreds of throats at the annual game between the Elmwood and Holwell schools, as the Freshmen prepared to clash in their gridiron battle.

The game was to take place on the Elmwood grounds, and both teams were out for practice. The crowds were beginning to arrive, and the bands were playing.

"Say, there's a mob here all right," remarked Jack to Tom. "A raft of people."

"Yes. I hope we win."

"Oh, sure we will. Don't get nervous. I only wish Bert was at quarter instead of Sam Heller."

"So do I, but it can't be helped. I guess it will be all right."

"Line up!"

It was the final call. The preliminaries had been all arranged, the goals chosen, and the practice balls called in. Elmwood was to kick off, and the new yellow pigskin was handed to her burly centre, who was poising it on a little mound of earth in the middle of the field.

"Ready?" asked the official.

"Ready!" answered both captains.

The whistle shrilled out its signal, and the toe of the big centre met the ball squarely. It was well kicked into the Holwell territory.

The full-back on the latter team caught it skillfully, and started to return with it, well protected by interference, but Jack Fitch worked his way through it, and tackled his man hard.

"Good! Good!" screamed the Elmwood enthusiasts, and then the first scrimmage was prepared for.

I am not going to describe for you that game in detail, for it formed but a small part in the life of Tom Fairfield. Sufficient to say that the gridiron battle was fairly even, and that at the end of the third quarter the score was a tie.

"But we've got to win!" declared the Elmwood captain, during the rest period. "We've got to."

"And we will, if there's a change made," declared Jack Fitch boldly.

"What do you mean?"

"I mean that Tom Fairfield isn't getting a fair show."

"Oh, Jack!" exclaimed Tom.

"That's right! You're not!" declared his chum. "Sam hasn't called on you three times during the game. It's been all wing shift plays, or place kicks, or forward passes, or fake kicks or something like that. Why can't we have some straight, old-fashioned football, with a rush of the half-back through tackle and guard or centre? Tom's a good ground-gainer."

"I've played him as much as I saw proper," snapped Sam.

"You have not!" declared Jack hotly.

"Easy, boys," cautioned the coach. "There must be no personal feeling. Perhaps some straight football would go well, Heller."

"All right, I'll give it to 'em."

The whistle blew to start the last quarter.

"Remember, boys, a touchdown will do the trick, and win the game!" pleaded the Elmwood captain.

"Look out for yourself, Tom," cautioned Jack.

"Why?"

"Because Sam is just mad enough to make you fumble the ball and spoil a play. Then he'll accuse you of losing the game."

"I'll watch out."

The play was resumed. It was give and take, hammer and tongs, with the best players making the most gains. The ball was slowly forced down the field toward the Holwell goal.

"Touchdown! Touchdown!" screamed the supporters of our hero's college, and there were many of them.

"Seven, eleven, thirty-three, Elmwood! Eight—nine—twenty-one!" called Sam.

It was the signal for the full-back to take the ball through centre. It was almost the last chance, for the time was nearly up, and Tom had not been given a single opportunity that quarter. His heart burned against his enemy; yet what could he do?

The quarter-back dropped his hands as a signal for the centre to snap the ball back. Sam caught it fairly, and turned to pass it to the full-back. Then, that always fatal element in football developed. There was a fumble. The ball was dropped.

"Grab it! Fall on it!" yelled half a dozen Holwell players.

The Elmwood line wavered. Could it hold?

Tom Fairfield, a mist before his eyes, saw the pigskin rolling toward him. He picked it up on the jump. In another moment Jack Fitch and Joe Rooney, his guard, had torn a hole in the opposing line.

"Come on, Tom!" yelled Jack hoarsely.

And Tom, with lowered head, with the ball held close to his breast, plunged into the line. He hit it hard. It yielded. He went through with a rush, pushed by Jack and Joe. Then, seeing but a single man between himself and the coveted goal, he rushed for it.

All but the opposing full-back had been drawn in at the sight of the fumble, and the chance to secure the ball. Tom rushed at this lone player.

There was a shock. Tom reeled, but managed to retain his footing. He shoved the full-back aside, and ran on.

"Oh, great!" he heard hundreds yell. "Go on! Go on!"

How he ran! It was the opportunity for which he had waited. In spite of Sam Heller it had come to him. Over the white chalk marks Tom scudded, until, with panting breath, with a heart that seemed bursting, and with eyes that scarcely saw, he fell over the last line, and planted the ball between the goal posts, making the winning touchdown. The other players—his own and his opponents—straggled up to the last mark. The whistle blew, ending the game.

"Oh wow!" shrilled hundreds of voices. "Elmwood! Elmwood! Elmwood forever!"

"Tom, you won the game! You won the game!" yelled Jack in his chum's ear, as Tom got up, holding his foot on the ball. "You won in spite of Sam!"

"I—I'm glad—of—it!" panted Tom, scarcely able to breathe even yet, for he had run hard.

CHAPTER X

A COWARD'S TRICK

"Three cheers for Fairfield!"

"Rah! Rah! Rah!—Elmwood!"

"Three cheers for Holwell!"

There were shouts, cries and cheers of joy at the victory on the part of our hero's followers, while there was corresponding gloom in the camp of their unsuccessful rivals.

"Great work, old man!" complimented Tom's captain. "You did the trick for us!"

"It was an accident. I just managed to get the ball, and run," explained Tom.

"Lucky for us you did. It was an accident that might have counted heavily against us. What was the matter with you, Sam, in passing the ball?"

"Aw, it wasn't my fault. It slipped. Anyhow our full-back had his hands on it, and he dropped it."

"I did not!" declared that player. "You didn't pass it to me fairly."

"That'll do!" interrupted the captain sharply. "We don't want any quarrels. Besides, we won the game."

Tom was surrounded by a joyous crowd of his chums, and other admirers, as the team raced from the field, and the throng of spectators filed out of the stands.

"Well, how do you feel?" asked Jack of his chum, as they were in their room together, after a refreshing bath in the gymnasium.

"Great! I expect I'll be a little lame and stiff tomorrow though. Somebody gave me a beaut dig in the ribs."

"And I guess our whole team, and half of the other one, was piled on me at one stage of the game," remarked Jack ruefully, as he rubbed his back reflectively. "But it was a glorious win all right. And how you did run, Tom!"

"I just had to, to make that touchdown." And then the two boys fell to talking of the game, playing it all over again in detail.

"I just thought Sam would be mean enough not to give you a chance," remarked Jack.

"Oh, maybe it wasn't intentional," replied our hero, who did not like to think ill of anyone.

"Get out! Of course it was. Ask any of the fellows. But he fooled himself. That fumble spoiled his plans, and you grabbed your opportunity."

"And the ball too," added Tom, as there came a knock on their door.

"Come!" called Jack, and Bert Wilson and George Abbot entered.

"Came to pay our respects," spoke Bert. "How does it feel to be hero? Aren't your ears burning, with the way the fellows are talking about you?"

"Not exactly."

"Why should his ears burn?" asked George. "Is it because he—"

"Now you quit, or I'll fire the dictionary at you," threatened Bert. "I told you I'd bring you in on one condition, and that was that you wouldn't be a question box."

"But I just wanted to know," pleaded George.

"Then look it up in an encyclopedia," directed Jack, with a laugh. "I'm not going to answer any more questions."

"I hope you get a chance next game," said Tom to Bert. "Maybe you will after the fumble Sam made."

And Bert did. For there was a conference between the Freshman captain and coach that night, which resulted in Sam being sent back to the scrub. He protested mightily.

"It wasn't my fault—that fumble," he declared.

"I think it was," spoke the coach. "Anyhow you didn't run the team as well as I thought you would. Why, you didn't give Fairfield half a chance, and he showed what he could do when he did get a show."

"Aw, he can't play football."

"I think he can. Anyhow, you'll shift back, but if you do good work I'll play you on the regular team again before the season is over." And with this Sam had to be content.

Football practice was resumed on Monday, and the team seemed to do better with the change in quarter-backs. There was a match in the middle of the week, and again Elmwood won handily, Jack Fitch distinguishing himself by a long run, while Tom made some star tackles, once saving a touchdown by catching the player a short distance from the goal.

"I'll get even with Fairfield yet!" threatened Sam to Nick. "He needn't think he can run things here."

"Go in and do him," advised his crony. "Can't you pick a quarrel with him, and have it out?"

"I'll try. If you see a chance, sail in and lick him."

"I will," promised Nick, but Sam's chance came sooner than he expected, or, rather, he made the opportunity.

There is a certain fine powder, a sort of a pepper-snuff so fine that it can not be seen floating about, yet which, if scattered about a room, will irritate the eyes, nose and throat in a marked degree. Sam bought some of this powder, and making it up into a small paper parcel, he watched his chance to slip it into Tom's handkerchief pocket.

"He'll pull it out in class," Sam explained to Nick, "and set the whole room to sneezing. I'll try and have him do it in Latin recitation, and Skeel won't do a thing to him, for Tom sits in the front row, and the prof. will see him."

"Suppose Fairfield catches you?"

"I'll take care that he doesn't," declared Sam, and he was lucky enough to bring about his cowardly trick undetected. As the students went into the Latin class, presided over by Professor Skeel, Sam slipped the sneezing powder into Tom's pocket, on top of his handkerchief. It was quickly done, and, in the press, our hero never noticed it. Then Sam quickly joined one of his classmates, with whom he was more or less thick, to prevent detection.

The recitation was about half over, and Tom, who had been called on, had made a failure, for a very hard question, and one he had never dreamed would be brought up in class, was asked him.

"Remain after the session, and write me out fifty lines of Cæsar," ordered the mean instructor. Tom shut his laps grimly. A little later he pulled out his handkerchief, and, as might have been expected, the powder flew out, scattering from the paper. A few moments later a boy began to sneeze, and soon the whole room was doing it—even the professor.

Now Professor Skeel was no simpleton, if he was mean, and he at once detected the irritating powder. He realized at once that some one had done it for a trick, and he had seen the paper fall from Tom's pocket, as the stuff scattered.

"Fairfield!" he exclaimed angrily, "did you scatter that powder?"

"Not intentionally, sir."

"What do you mean?"

"I mean that I did not know it was there. Some one must have put it in my pocket for a joke."

"Nonsense! Do you expect me to believe that?" the professor asked sharply of Tom.

"It's the truth, sir."

"Preposterous! I don't believe you!"

"Sir!" exclaimed our hero, for he was not in the habit of being told that he spoke an untruth.

"Don't contradict me!" stormed the teacher. "I say you did it on purpose—er—a-ker-choo! On purpose—ker-choo! I have known it to be done before, in other classes, but never in mine. I will have no nonsense! Ker-choo!"

The professor was having hard work to talk, for he sneezed quite often, as, in fact, did every one in the class.

"This foolishness will have to stop!" he declared. "I am certain you put that powder in your own pocket, Fairfield."

"I did not, sir."

"Ha! Did any one here put that powder in Fairfield's pocket?" asked the professor.

Naturally the guilty Sam did not answer.

"There, you see!" exclaimed Mr. Skeel, triumphantly. "I knew you did it—ker-choo! But I have no doubt others may have been implicated, and I will punish the whole class. You will all of you write me out a hundred lines of Cæsar."

"That is not fair, sir," spoke Tom boldly.

"What! You dare to tell me that!" stormed Mr. Skeel.

"It is not fair," insisted Tom. "Either I alone am responsible, which I deny, or some one else is. I assure you, sir, that no one in the class entered with me into any trick to do this thing."

"I don't believe you. The whole class will be punished unless the guilty one confesses—and that includes you!" and the professor looked angrily at Tom.

Sam, of course, would not admit his part in the affair, and as it was impossible to have the class remain longer in the powder-infested room, the students were dismissed. But Professor Skeel would not remit the punishment.

"Say, this is tough luck—to have to write out all that Latin, for something we didn't do," complained Frank Nelson.

"I should say so," added Harry Morse. "Why don't you own up to it, Fairfield, and save our hides."

"Because I didn't do it intentionally."

"Honestly?"

"Of course."

"Say, if Tom says he didn't do it, he didn't," declared Jack.

"I guess that's right," agreed Harry. "Excuse me, Tom," and, to the credit of Tom's classmates, one and all expressed their belief in his innocence. That is, all but Sam, and he kept quiet, avoiding our hero. But, to ward off suspicion, Sam growled louder than anyone about the task.

"I'd like to get hold of the fellow who used that powder," complained Ed. Ward.

"You won't have to look far for him, I guess," said Jack, in a voice that only Tom heard.

"Do you think Sam did it?" asked Tom.

"I sure do. But you want to be certain of your proof against him before you accuse him!"

"I will," declared Tom. "I'll do a bit of detective work."

But he had no clews to work on, and, though he was sure his enemy had made him and the others suffer, he could prove nothing, for the paper in which the powder was wrapped was blank.

CHAPTER XI

A CLASS WARNING

"Well, if any of you young gentlemen have any more powder to scatter around, you had better do it, and have done with it," remarked Professor Skeel a day or so later, when Tom and his chums came in to recite. "Only if you do," he added sarcastically, "the punishment I meted out before will be doubled, and, in case the offense is repeated a third time, I will go on doubling the task, if necessary in arithmetical progression."

He looked at the lads, with a sneering smile on his face. There were mutterings of discontent from all, save perhaps Sam Heller, for the lads felt not only the injustice of the uncalled-for remarks, but the former punishment still rankled in their minds.

"No one seems inclined to take advantage of my offer," went on Professor Skeel, "so we will go on with the lesson. Fairfield, you may begin. We'll see if you are prepared."

Tom was, fortunately, and it seemed not only to him, but to some of the others, as if the teacher was displeased. Very likely he would have been glad of a chance to punish Tom. But he did not get it—at least that day.

"Unmannerly brute!" murmured Tom, as he sat down. "I'll pay you back yet. Not because of what you did to me, but because you're unfair to the rest of the class."

Tom hated unfairness, and he also felt that, in a way, he was to blame for the punishment the class had unjustly suffered. He had not been able to learn anything about how the powder came to be put in his pocket, though he suspected Heller more than ever, as he saw how vindictive the Freshman bully was toward him.

"I almost wish he'd pick a fight with me," thought Tom. "Then I could give him what he deserves."

But Sam saw no chance of doing any further harm to the lad whom he hated with so little cause.

"Why can't you think of something to help me out?" Sam asked of his crony.

"Think of something yourself," retorted Nick. "I've got my own troubles. We're going to haze the Freshmen tonight, and I'm on the committee of rules and regulations," and he laughed.

"You are? Then this is my chance! Come over here where we can talk," and the bully led his crony to one side.

This talk followed the dismissal of Professor Skeel's Latin class, during which nothing had occurred save that the instructor took every chance of insulting the students.

"Say, if this keeps up much longer, we'll have to do something, Jack," declared Tom, as they proceeded on to another recitation.

"That's right. But what can we do?"

"Oh, I'm going to think of something. I wish we could haze him."

"So do I. But I guess we'll be hazed ourselves first."

"How's that?"

"Why it's this week that the Sophs get after us. We may expect them any night now. Going to crawl?"

"I am not! Might as well have it over with."

"That's what I say."

Though Tom and his Freshmen chums rather expected the advent of their traditional enemies, the Sophomores, they hardly looked for visits that same night, and so, when a knock came on the door of the room occupied by Tom and Jack, they opened it unsuspectingly.

"Here are two!" exclaimed a voice, as several masked figures entered. "We're in luck! Grab 'em!"

The orders of the ringleader were obeyed. Tom and Jack could not tell who their captors were.

"I say, Tom, shall we fight 'em?" asked Jack, always ready for a battle.

"No, what's the use—in here?" asked Tom significantly.

"Ha! Scrappers, eh?" remarked another Sophomore. "You're the kind we're looking for!"

"And maybe you'll get more than you want!" exclaimed Tom. Neither he nor Jack resisted as they were led forth. It was a sort of unwritten rule that no fighting against the hazers should take place in the dormitories, as property was likely to be damaged.

"Wait until we get in the open!" whispered Tom to Jack, as they were being led down stairs. "Then we'll upset 'em if we can, and run. They don't look to be very husky."

"That's right," agreed Tom's chum.

"Ha! No plotting!" cried the ringleader, giving Tom a dig in the ribs.

"I'll give you that back with interest when I get the chance," murmured our hero.

Other parties of hazers made their appearance in the corridor, some leading Bert Wilson and George Abbot.

"Where are you taking me? What are you going to do? Is this allowed?" fired George at his captors.

"Sure it's allowed, you little question mark!" exclaimed a Sophomore. "Trot along now."

Tom and his chums were led over the campus. They could see other little groups of prisoners in like plight, and the Sophomores, all of whom wore masks, gathered together with their captives.

"To the river!" ordered the ringleaders. "We'll make 'em wade a bit."

"Oh, they're going to duck us!" whimpered George. "I wonder why they do it?"

"Oh, there goes Why!" exclaimed Jack. "He can't keep still."

"They're not going to duck me!" murmured Tom. "Come on, Jack, now's our chance. Make a break!"

It was the best chance Tom had seen, and, with a sudden push, and a putting out of his foot, he tripped the lad who had hold of his arm. Then, with a well-directed punch, he paid him back for the dig in the ribs. Tom was free to run.

"Come on, Jack!" he called. His chum, performing a like trick, was also free, and their two captors were down on the ground. But the flight did not go unnoticed.

"Two are loose! Grab the two Freshies!" yelled the lads who had held Tom and Jack. The cry was taken up, and some of the Sophomores, who had no Freshmen to take care of, ran after the two chums. Our heroes might have gotten away but for the fact that two lads, masked, who were coming across the campus to join their fellows, saw them, and waited to catch the two fleeing ones.

Tom and Jack tried to dodge, but could not. There was a clash, and Jack was caught. In a moment other Sophomores came up, and had him. Tom was struggling with his captor.

"Take that!" cried the latter, when, finding he could not subdue Tom, he struck our hero a blow in the face.

"I won't take that from any one!" cried Tom fiercely. "Hazing customs or not!" He retaliated, and with such good measure that he knocked the other down. The black mask came off in the fall, and it was light enough for Tom to see Sam Heller.

"You!" he cried. "You're not a Sophomore! You have no right to haze!"

"This is my second year here. I'm a Sophomore by rights!" growled Sam, much put out that his trick had been discovered. "I'll get even with you, too!"

In his rage he leaped up and rushed at Tom. It was just the chance the other wanted, and our hero promptly knocked Sam down again. He was wild with rage. By this time a knot of Sophomores surrounded Tom.

"Hold on there, Fresh!" cried some one who seemed to be in authority. "This won't do, you know. You shouldn't fight back when you're being hazed."

"Has a Freshman the right to help the Sophs haze us?" demanded Tom, as he recognized Bruce Bennington in the objector. "Here's Sam Heller, of our class, joining against us."

"Is that so?" asked Bruce in surprise. With some other Seniors he had come out to see the fun. "That's not allowed, you know, Wendell," he said, turning to the leader of the Second year lads.

"I didn't know Heller was here," replied Wendell. "That's straight. He has no right. We beg your pardon, Fairfield. Sam, how did this happen?" Wendell was justly indignant.

"Well, I claim I'm a Sophomore, and I would be if I had a fair show. I thought I had a right to help haze." Sam was whining now, like all cowards when found out. His trick, which he had formed with the aid of Nick, had failed. The two had planned to get Jack and Tom off alone, during the general excitement over the hazing, and thrash them.

"You're not a Soph, and you can't do any hazing," declared Wendell decidedly. "You ought to be hazed yourself, and you would be, only you got yours last year. Come along now, Fairfield, and take what's coming to you."

"All right," agreed Tom good-naturedly. He was satisfied with what he had done to Sam. The crowd of Sophomores was now so large that there was no chance for our hero and his chum to escape.

"Take your medicine, Fairfield," advised Bruce with a laugh. "It won't be very bad."

"All right," said Tom again, and he and Jack were led back to their luckless mates, the little group of Seniors following.

The hazing was not very severe. The Freshmen were made to wade in the river up to their knees, and then, with coats turned inside out, forced to dance in a ring, while the Sophomores laughed their delight, and played mouth organs. Some few were tossed in blankets, and much horse play was indulged in. But the discovery of Heller's trick rather discomfited the second year lads, and they felt that there was a little blight on their class. Otherwise the hazing might have been more severe.

"Now then, form in line, and give three cheers for the Sophs, and you can go home to your beds," declared Wendell. "Only remember, every Freshman must wear his cap backwards every time he comes on the campus, for the next two weeks, and salute every Sophomore he meets, under penalty of being hazed over again. Remember! Now for the cheers!"

They were given, and the hazing was over. No one had been much annoyed by it, save perhaps Sam Heller.

"It didn't work," he grumbled to Nick, later that night. "We had a fight, though."

"Did you lick him?" asked Nick, who had been separated from his crony during the fracas with Tom.

"I sure did."

"How'd you get that bruise near your eye?" asked Nick.

"Oh—er—I—sort of fell," stammered Sam. The bruise was where Tom had hit him.

And thus the hazing of Tom's Freshman class passed into history.

Several weeks passed, and our hero came to like the school more and more. He made many new chums, and no more enemies, though Sam and Nick disliked him more than ever, and thought bitter thoughts, and devised endless schemes to "get even," as they expressed it, though the debt was on their side. But, though they annoyed Tom and his chum often, the latter as often got back at them in hearty fashion.

Tom heard from his parents, that they had arrived safely, and they said the business was going on satisfactorily. The weather was getting colder each day, and the boys began to have thoughts of skating and ice boating as soon as the river should be frozen over. The football season had closed.

Then, unexpectedly, there came another clash with Professor Skeel. In Latin class one day several students came unprepared, and failed in reciting.

"We'll stop right here!" exclaimed the professor. "It is evident to me that an organized attempt to miss in Latin is under way. I shall double the usual number of lines that you are all to write out. Perhaps that will teach you not to trifle with me."

Several protested at this, saying that the reason for their failure was additional work in other classes. Others, who had not failed, declared that it was manifestly unfair to make them suffer with the rest.

"Silence!" snapped the professor. "You may stay here until your tasks are done," and he prepared to leave the room, intending to send a monitor to take charge of the lads.

"Say, this is rank injustice!" exclaimed Jack.

"It sure is," came from Tom. "And the ice on the river is thick enough for skating, I believe. If we didn't have to stay here we could cut the next lecture and have some fun."

"We sure could. What'll we do?"

"Let's haze Skeel!" suggested Bert Wilson, for there was no one in authority in the room now.

"Let's send him a warning," suggested Tom. "We'll write it out in Latin, and threaten to go on a strike, or burn him in effigy if he doesn't act more fair. How's that?"

"Good!" exclaimed several. "Tom, you write out the notice."

"I will!" agreed our hero, and then a monitor came in, and silence was enforced. But Tom, after hurrying through the prescribed number of lines of prose, began work on the warning.

CHAPTER XII

A RUNAWAY ICEBOAT

"How are we going to get it to him?" asked Bert Wilson, as the Latin class, its members having finished their punishment, filed out on the campus.

"Mail it to him," suggested Jack.

"No, leave it at his door," advised Henry Miller.

"Huh! Who'd do it?" asked George Abbot.

"There you go again, Why!" exclaimed Tom with a laugh, as he passed around the warning he had composed.

"Well, I mean who would have the nerve to go up and leave that at Skeel's door?" went on the small lad. "I wouldn't."

"I would!" declared Tom. "I'm tired of being imposed upon!"

"And so am I!" exclaimed Jack. "I'm with you. Let's get a lot of Freshmen, tog up in masks, or with pillow cases over our heads, and leave the warning at his door. That'll make him be more decent, I guess."

"All right," agreed Tom. "We'll do it."

That same night Tom, and several bold spirits, with pillow cases, or white cloths over their coats, slipped from the dormitory where the Freshmen lived, moved and had their being. Tom carried his warning.

It was in Latin, more or less accurate, and in plain terms demanded on the part of Professor Skeel a more tolerant attitude toward the Freshman class, or, failure would be met with a burning in effigy of the disliked instructor. And the boys meant it, too.

"All ready now?" asked Tom as he and his chums, in the dark shadows of a thick hedge around Mr. Skeel's house had adjusted their head-coverings. "All ready?"

"Lead on!" whispered Jack. "Who's going to knock at the door?"

"I will," agreed Tom. "We'll go around to his 'study,' as he calls it. It's got a door opening directly into the garden, and he'll answer the knock himself."

Advancing from amid group of his chums a little later, with the warning held in the cleft end of a long stick, Tom knocked on Mr. Skeel's door. The professor was in his study, poring over some book, and laying new traps, in the way of difficult questions, for his pupils.

"Who's there?" he cried sharply, at the sound of Tom's rap.

A groan was the answer.

"What nonsense is this?" demanded Professor Skeel, as he rose from his chair.

"If those are students they'll pay dearly for this nonsense!" he was heard to exclaim, as he opened the door. The sight of the white-robed figures, with one standing out from the others, holding forth a letter in a cleft stick, was a distinct surprise to the professor.

"What is the meaning of this?" he cried. "Who are you? I demand to know!"

Groans were his only answer, and Tom waved the letter before the professor's face. In very wonderment the instructor took it and then, with a final series of groans, Tom and the others turned and hurried away.

"Come back. I demand that you return. Take those silly cloths from your heads, and let me see who you are!" cried Professor Skeel, but our hero and his chums knew better than to tarry.

"Halt!" cried the professor. He started after the lads, but, as he reached the bottom step he tripped on a stick, and fell and, as he had on light slippers, the contact of his toes with the ground was anything but comfortable.

Uttering an exclamation of anger, the professor went back into his study with the letter, while Tom and his chums hurried to their rooms, getting to them undetected.

"What's this?" burst out Professor Skeel, as he read Tom's Latin warning. "They demand better treatment! Burn me in effigy, eh? Why this is a threat! A threatening letter! I'll have the entire Freshman class suspended! I shall see Dr. Meredith at once!"

In his anger he did go over and see the head master, showing him the letter.

"Hum! Well," mused Doctor Meredith. "That is a sort of threat, Professor Skeel, but—er—would not it be well to—er—to grant the class a few more privileges? Remember they are first year lads, unused to the discipline of a college, and, therefor, not to be dealt with too harshly. Could you not grant their request?"

"What? My dear sir! Grant a request coupled with a threat? Never! I demand the suspension of the entire Freshman class, until the perpetrators of this outrage are discovered, and then I demand their expulsion. Why, Doctor Meredith, they had the audacity to call on me, disguised. On me! They had the effrontery to threaten me in a miserably composed Latin scrawl. Me! I demand the suspension of the entire class!"

"Hum! Well, I'm afraid I can't do that," said the head master. "I shall take this under advisement, and act in the morning. But I can't suspend the whole class. They are not all guilty, I'm sure," and nothing the irate professor said could change this decision.

In the morning Doctor Meredith referred to the matter, not half as strongly, however, as Professor Skeel thought should have been done. There was no threat to suspend the class, and all the doctor did was to suggest that different measures be taken in the future. He also asked those engaged in the affair to make themselves known.

"As if we would!" exclaimed Tom, later. And I hardly believe Doctor Meredith expected that the lads would. He had been a college master for many years, and he knew boys, which Professor Skeel did not.

"Oh, but we'll get it in Latin class," predicted Jack. "We'd better all be prepared today."

And they all were, very well prepared, but that did not save them from an angry tongue-lashing, in which the professor, on his own account, demanded to know those who had been instrumental in writing and bringing the warning.

Of course no one answered, and, as Tom had taken the precaution to print out the letter, his handwriting was not recognized. Every device, however, that an angry and bullying teacher could bring to bear, was used on the class. But no one failed, and no punishment could be inflicted. Though had the professor been able to use his power he would have administered corporal punishment to all the Freshmen.

The result was, however, that the Latin recitation was perfect, and, in his heart the instructor was just a little bit afraid of the threat of burning him in effigy. So, in a few days he did mend his ways somewhat, and the class began to feel that Tom's plan had worked wonders. But the end was not yet.

"Well, Tom, I've had enough of this!" exclaimed Jack, one cold afternoon, when the two chums had been "boning" away in their room for some time. "Let's go hire that iceboat you were talking of, and have a sail on the river. I guess she's frozen over thick enough."

"I'm with you!" and Tom tossed his book to one side. "Let's get George, Bert and some of the others."

Some days before Tom had discovered that the man of whom the lads hired their rowboats, had a couple of ice craft for rent, and he had engaged one for the first good day.

A little later Tom and several of his chums, including Jack, were on their way to the frozen river, lessons being over for the day.

"Well, where are you bound for?" asked Bruce Bennington, as he met Tom and the others near the stream.

"Ice boating. Come along," invited Tom.

"Thanks. I believe I will. I was going for a skate, but somehow, I don't feel like exerting myself."

There was a look of worriment still on the Senior's face, and he talked as though the trouble that was worrying him had not passed away. Tom wanted to help him, but knew it was best to say nothing.

A part of the river, where the water was not so deep, nor the current under the ice so swift as elsewhere, had been set aside by the school authorities as the place where the students might skate. They were forbidden to use the steel runners elsewhere, as a matter of safety, and, as the skating course was plenty long enough, none of the lads ventured on the part of the river where the ice boats were used. In fact the presence of those craft, of which there were several, made it necessary that the numerous skaters keep clear of them.

The place where Tom hired the iceboat was quite a distance from the skating course, and, in consequence of a bend in the river, none of the other pupils, who were indulging in sports on the steel blades, were in sight. There was one iceboat out on the broad surface of the river as our hero and his chums arrived.

"Know how to sail one?" asked Bruce, as he took his place in the shallow box that served as a sort of cockpit, while some of the boys perched on the runners.

"Fairly well," replied Tom, and soon they were skimming over the slippery surface, with Tom at the helm. It was great sport, and they liked it immensely.

"This is fine!" exclaimed Bruce, with sparkling eyes, and something of a return of his old manner. "It beats skating!" and he kicked his skates that he had tossed into the box near him.

"Oh, skating's all right!" declared Tom, as he changed the course slightly. "We'll have some skating races soon, won't we?"

"Yes, it's about time for them," answered the Senior.

After sailing for several miles Tom decided to put up a sort of auxiliary sail on the boat, to get more speed. It was fitted to a short bamboo mast, about five feet high.

"You'll all have to get out while I fix it," suggested Tom, as he let the wind spill out of the big sail, and brought the boat up with a turn, while it gradually came to a stop.

They piled out, stamping up and down to warm their rather benumbed legs and feet. Tom and Jack were soon putting up the little sail.

"I've got to whittle down the end of the mast to make it fit in," declared Tom after a trial. "Lend me your knife, Jack."

Bruce had put on his skates for a little turn while he waited, and the others were racing up and down. Tom and Jack were working over the auxiliary sail, standing a short distance away from the iceboat, when there came a sudden puff of wind. The main sheet became caught, the big sail filled, and a moment later the empty iceboat was racing over the smooth, frozen river at dangerous speed!

CHAPTER XIII

THE SKATING RACE

"Look at that!" cried Jack.

"See it go!" shouted Bert.

"How did it happen to get away?" the ever-questioning George wanted to know.

"By Jove!" murmured Bruce. "He'd ask questions if it was the end of the world. He'd want to know why it hadn't happened before."

"Wow!" came from Tom, as he started after the disappearing iceboat. "That's bad! I'm responsible for it." He started off on a run, as though he could catch the skimming craft.

"You'll never get her!" yelled Bruce to him. He had taken off his skates, and hurried up beside Tom.

"I've got to get her!" cried our hero. "She may run against the bank and go to smash."

"You can't stop her. She's too far off. Look at her veer! She'll capsize in another minute!"

Indeed the unguided craft was slewing about, making quick turns and big circles as the wind blew her. Then Tom cried out:

"I'm going to catch her. Lend me your skates, Bruce."

"You can't skate as fast as that boat is going!"

"I can try. Besides I'm not going to do all skating."

"What then?" asked Jack, curious to know what scheme his chum had in his mind.

"This!" and Tom pointed to the small sail he had been going to rig on the craft when she went off by herself. "I can hold this at my back by the mast, and the wind will blow me along."

"Good!" cried Bruce, who understood. "That's the idea Fairfield, here are my skates."

Tom soon had clamped them on his feet, and then, holding the improvised sail at his back, he headed for the runaway iceboat. The sail was almost like the regular ones skaters use.

Tom soon developed great speed, for the wind was strong and directly at his back. The others started to run after him. The iceboat was some distance ahead, but Tom was rapidly overhauling her.

"I'll get her before she goes to smash," he murmured hopefully. The boat suddenly heeled over, and Tom thought surely she was going to capsize. But she righted, and then went off on a new tack. Tom saw his chance.

"I can quarter across and get aboard, if she doesn't veer again!" he cried, and he altered his course. Nearer and nearer he came to the iceboat, until he saw that he would soon pass her. "If only she doesn't veer around," he murmured hopefully.

Fortunately, however, the wind held in that direction for a few minutes, and the main sheet of the sail was caught in such a way as to hold the craft steady.

"Now to do some skating on my own hook!" cried Tom, as he cast aside the little sail. He struck out with all his strength and speed, and, as he came close to the boat, with a leap and a spring he hurled himself into the blanket-covered cockpit, landing with a thud.

It was the work of but a moment to seize the rudder, and put the boat about, so that she was in control, though even as Tom did this she nearly capsized.

"Whoa, now!" he called, as to a restive horse, and then, settling himself down, he sent the boat back on a series of tacks to pick up his chums.

"Say, did you see him skate!" exclaimed Bert Wilson in admiration, as he called attention to the burst of speed on Tom's part.

"I should say yes," admitted Jack. "If we have a race I'll back Tom."

"He looks like a winner," commented Bruce quietly.

Tom brought the iceboat up to his chums, and they got aboard. Jack steered while Tom took off the skates he had not had time to remove, and then he went to where he had dropped the little sail.

"I guess we'll get along without it," he remarked. "We're going fast enough."

"I never thought you'd get the boat in time," spoke Bruce admiringly. "Where'd you learn to skate, Fairfield?"

"Oh, I could make pretty good time ever since I was a small lad, but I sort of broke my record today, I guess."

They were soon back at the boathouse, having talked on the way of the little accident and of Tom's skill.

"You'll enter for the class races, won't you?" inquired Reddy Burke of Tom, a little later, when Bruce had told of the Freshman's skill.

"I'll be glad to."

"They'll come off in about a week if the ice holds," went on the red-haired athlete.

Practice for the skating races was soon under way. The affair was to settle the championship of the school. Later, intercollegiate contests would be held.

"Going to try?" asked Nick of his crony, when the notice of the ice sports was posted. "I hear Fairfield is a wonder."

"What do I care? I can skate some myself, and if I can't win, maybe I can spoil his chances."

"How?"

"Oh, I haven't made up my mind yet."

It was a cold, clear day, the ice was firm and smooth, and it was just right for a skating race. The elimination trials had been held, and the representatives of each class selected. There were four each from the Freshmen, Sophomore, Junior and Senior divisions. Tom, of course, was picked, and so was Jack, and, somewhat to the surprise of many, Sam Heller also represented the first year lads.

"Look out for him," advised Jack to his chum, when they were getting ready. "If he skates near enough to you he may try some mean trick."

"I'll watch out, but I'm not worried."

"I wonder if he'd be mean enough to squeal to our Latin prof. about the warning letter you wrote?" went on Jack. "I've often thought of that. He's equal to it."

"Oh, I don't believe Heller would dare do a thing like that," spoke Tom. "I'm not alarmed. There, I guess my skates are sharp enough," for the two had been putting an extra edge on the steel runners in anticipation of the contest.

There was a big crowd present to watch the skaters, who were lined up, receiving their last instructions from the officials. Clamps were being tightened, straps made more snug, and the last little attentions being given.

"All ready?" called the starter.

"Ready!" answered the lads in turn.

"Look out for Sam. He's quite near you," warned Jack to his chum, in a low voice. Tom nodded and looked across at the bully, who had his head turned away.

"Go!" cried the starter, and his pistol cracked out on the frosty air.

CHAPTER XIV

WINNING AGAINST ODDS

The skaters were off together, almost like a line of well-drilled soldiers on the double-quick, and, as they glided forward, there came a shrill burst of cheers from the student spectators.

"Rah! Rah! Freshmen! Elmwood Freshmen!" cried the members of that class, to urge on their comrades.

"Boom! Boom! Boomity-boom Seniors! Siss!" came the peculiar cry of the four-year lads.

"Sophomore! Sophomore!Rah! Rah! Rah!Going like a trolley car!"

That was the second year boys cheering.

Then came the call of the Juniors:

"June! June, beautiful June.We'll win the race and win it soon.Siss!Boom!Rah!Juniors!"

The line was a trifle broken now, as one or two forged ahead of the others, and among them was Tom. Yet he was holding himself in check, and narrowly watching the others, for the race was not a short one, and he knew the danger of getting winded too early in it, and spending his strength so that he had none left for a final spurt.

Jack was even with his chum, though he was not as good a skater as was our hero. Sam Heller was a little behind, but in practice he had done well, and Tom knew that in his enemy he had a dangerous rival.

Bruce Bennington was skating well, the only one of the Seniors who seemed to stand a chance, while a member each of the Junior and Sophomore class was up in the front now.

"Everyone is holding back," said Jack to Tom.

"Yes, waiting for a break. I've a good notion to give it to 'em, and take a chance."

"Don't you do it. Let some one else set the pace. Hold back. We want to win this race for the Freshman class, and we're depending on you."

"Hope I don't disappoint you. There goes Blaisdell for the Juniors. Come on!"

One of the skaters had spurted and at once the others increased their speed to keep up to him. The race was now on in earnest, and soon half thedistance was covered, with no one markedly in the lead. Several had dropped out, hopelessly distanced, but there were enough of each class left to make the result doubtful.

"I wonder what Sam is going to do?" mused Nick Johnson, as he watched his crony. "He'd better get busy."

The skaters had turned, and were coming back toward the starting point. They could hear the cheers of their comrades, and the cries of the followers of the various classes could be distinguished.

"Better hit it up, Tom," advised Jack.

"I will. Here goes!"

Tom struck out with more speed and power than he had previously used. He imagined he was once more chasing the runaway iceboat, and he gripped his fists and clenched his teeth as he made up his mind to win.

But, even as he spurted, others glided up, almost beside him, and one of them was Sam Heller. Tom watched out of the corner of his eye, and it seemed to him that Sam was edging over toward him.

"I wonder what he's doing that for?" mused Tom.

So near were they to the finish line now that the calls of the class cheerers came clearly through the cold, crisp air.

"Come on, Freshmen! Come on! Win! Win!"

"Don't let 'em beat you, Seniors!"

"Skate. Skate. Oh you Sophs!"

"Juniors forever. Juniors to the front!"

Thus the students cheered.

"I'm going to win!" whispered Tom fiercely to himself.

The finish line was a hundred feet away. Tom looked ahead, and saw a confused mass of excited spectators, waving flags and banners, tossing caps in the air, dancing about and uttering yells at the tops of their voices. He looked to left and right and saw on one side of him, Bruce Bennington, and, on the other, Sam Heller. Jack Fitch was not in sight.

"I guess Jack's out of it," mused Tom, regretfully.

He gathered himself for a final effort, and, just as he struck out with increased force he saw Sam lurch over toward him.

"Look out!" Tom yelled.

The bully returned no answer. He seemed to have lost control of himself. Nearer and nearer he glided toward Tom.

In vain did our hero try to get out of the way of what in a flash he knew to be an intentional attempt to foul him. But he could not escape without swerving so far to one side as to mean the loss of the race.

"Look out for yourself!" warned Tom, determined to give way no longer, and he braced himself for the shock.

It came an instant later, when Sam's skate struck Tom's, staggering him.

"Excuse me!" panted the bully, unnecessarily loud. "I couldn't help it!"

Tom said nothing, but he thought a lot.

Then he felt himself falling. There was but one thing to do, and Tom did it. He was staggering forward, trying in vain to remain upright long enough to cross the line. The only way he could do it was to gain more momentum than that caused by Sam's foul interference. That was to jump, and Tom did it.

Up in the air he rose, remembering the time he had cleared barrels on the ice in an obstacle race.

Up and up he went, fairly hurling himself forward. As he did so he had a confused glimpse of Sam Heller sprawling on the ice, and tumbling over and over. Tom also saw Bruce Bennington looking at him in astonishment. Our hero also had a glance at representatives of the Junior and Sophomore classes fairly doubled up in a desperate effort to win the race.

"But I'll do it! I'll do it, if I don't break a skate when I come down, or trip," thought Tom, desperately.

The jump had accomplished the very purpose for which the plucky Freshman intended it. Just as when you trip, and fall forward, if you can suddenly jump, and equalize the momentum given the upward part of our body, while overcoming the inertia of your feet, caused by the contact with some obstacle—just in this way Tom had jumped.

He saw the finish line but a few feet ahead. The next moment, amid a perfect riot of cheers, he came down with resounding force on the ice, his steel runners ringing out in the frosty air.

For a second he feared that he could not keep his balance, but by a desperate effort he did, and with great speed he slid across the mark, and fairly into the crowd of students bunched beyond it. Tom was unable to stop himself.

A quick glance showed that he was alone when he crossed the finish mark. He had won the race against big odds!

CHAPTER XV
MORE TROUBLE

"Freshmen win!"

"Rah, Freshmen! Elmwood forever! Freshmen win!"

"Hurray for Tom Fairfield!"

"And after a foul, too. He won after a foul!"

"Never mind. We won't claim it. Maybe it was an accident. Heller may be hurt!"

"Seniors Second! Bruce Bennington is second!"

These were only a few of the cries that greeted the achievement of our hero as he won the school race. He had come to a stop amid a knot of his classmates, who gathered about him, clasping him by the hand, clapping him on the back, and generally congratulating him.

"Great work, old man!"

"Magnificent jump!"

"How in the world did you do it?"

"I don't know myself," confessed Tom, with a laugh. "I just had to—that's all."

"Are you hurt, Tom?" demanded Jack, anxiously, as he skated up to his chum. "Did his skate hit your ankle?" for well he knew the agonizing pain that follows the blow of the point of a skate against that tender part of the foot.

"No, not a bit," replied Tom. "His skate just glanced off mine, but I'd have gone down if I hadn't jumped. Is Heller hurt?"

"I guess not much, though he's limping to the finish. It would serve him right if he was. He deliberately fouled you."

"I think so myself, but I'm not going to say anything."

"Well, maybe it's best. Class honor, you know."

The officials of the race were marking down the time, and formally declaring Tom the winner, with Bruce Bennington second and Peter Ranson, of the Sophomore class, third. The Juniors were not in the race at all, much to their disappointment.

"I—er—I presume your collision with Fairfield was an accident—was it not, Heller?" asked Professor Livingston Hammond, the fat and jolly professor who had acted as one of the officials. "We saw it from here."

"It was an accident—certainly," replied Sam, sharply. He had taken off his skates, and came limping up. "I could not help it. My skate struck a small piece of wood, and I slid over toward him. I tried to warn him, but it was too late. If anyone doubts my word—"

"No one dreamed of doubting you—or even mentioned it," interrupted Mr. Hammond with a smile, yet he looked at Sam narrowly.

"Three cheers for Professor Hammond!" called someone, and they were given with a will. Out on the fringe of spectators stood Professor Skeel, with a frown on his face. No one had cheered him, and he felt no elation that a member of his Freshman Latin class had won the race. In fact, there was a sneer on his face as he saw the ovation accorded to Tom.

"I more than half believe that he wrote that insulting and threatening letter to me," Professor Skeel muttered. "I must find out, and if he did—" a cruel smile played over his features. "Ah, there is some one else I must have a talk with!" he exclaimed as he saw Bruce Bennington walking along, swinging his skates. "Come here Bennington," he called, and the face of Bruce went rather white, and there was a nervous air in his manner, not to say a tinge of fear, as he approached the unpleasant instructor.

"Well, sir?" he asked.

"Are you ready to settle with me?" asked Professor Skeel, in a frosty tone.

"No, Professor, I'm sorry to say I am not."

"When will you be?"

"I can't say. Really, I am having it harder than you can imagine."

"Harder? Don't you suppose that I have my own troubles, too? Have you appealed to your folks?"

"No, and I'm not going to!" Bruce spoke fiercely.

"You may have to," and the Latin instructor's tone was threatening. "I shall not wait much longer, and if you do not make the appeal I shall do so myself."

"Oh, Professor Skeel, surely you wouldn't do that!"

"I certainly shall, unless you settle with me soon. I will wait but a little longer."

"Well, I'll see what I can do," spoke Bruce, wearily.

"You'd better," answered the professor significantly, as he turned aside.

Tom, coming along with Jack and some of his chums, heard the last words, though no one else seemed to have done so. He also noticed the threatening attitude of the Latin instructor, and was aware of the despondent attitude of the Senior student.

"I wish I knew what was up between them," mused Tom. "I would do a lot to help Bruce. Maybe it's some trouble about examination papers. And yet I know Bruce wouldn't be guilty of cheating, or anything like that. I wonder what it is?"

But Tom had little time to think by himself quietly, for his chums were jostling all about him, talking of the race, congratulating him over and over again, while some spoke significantly of Heller's action.

"Oh, forget that," advised Tom. "He came out of it worse than I did."

"I should say yes," agreed Jack. "He might have broken his leg trying a trick like that."

Tom's chums crowded into his room, and that night there was an impromptu and surreptitious little spread, held there in violation of the school rules.

Professor Skeel got word of it through one of the monitors, and went to notify Doctor Meredith.

"Hum, some of the Freshmen eating in the room of young Fairfield, eh?" murmured the good doctor.

"Yes. In direct violation of rule twenty-one. If you come with me now, we can catch them in the act."

"Hum. Yes! Let me see, didn't Fairfield win the skating race today, Professor Skeel?"

"He did, certainly, but I don't see what that has to do with it," snapped Mr. Skeel.

"Well, perhaps it has. I—er—I think—well, on the whole, I think I won't disturb the boys tonight, Professor Skeel."

"What! You will suffer a rule to be broken?"

"Well, in view of the facts, and under the circumstances, I guess it won't do the rule much harm," spoke the doctor dryly.

Professor Skeel threw up his hands helplessly, and walked off, muttering to himself. And Tom and his chums were not disturbed that night.

"But I'll take that Fairfield lad down a peg," the irate Latin instructor muttered as he went into his house. He sat up late that night, evolving a plan to discover who had sent him the threatening letter, and at last he exclaimed:

"I believe I have it. That will give me a clew. And then—!"

He smiled sourly as he took out the screed Tom had printed, and looked closely at it.

"I will find out who composed that!" he went on, "and when I do he shall suffer for it!"

The Freshman class little realized what it was in for at the hands of Professor Skeel.

It was a day or so after the great skating race, when the Freshmen filed into Latin recitation, that they became aware of something unusual in the air. Professor Skeel looked at them individually and collectively with a mocking smile on his face.

"He's got it in for some of us," murmured Tom to Jack.

"Silence!" exclaimed the instructor, banging a ruler on his desk. "I will permit no levity!"

The boys filed to their seats more than usually silent. The professor opened his book, and some one sneezed. It was a perfectly natural and unavoidable sneeze, yet it set off the mine that had been smouldering in the professor's breast for many days.

"Stop that!" he cried. "If I find that any more of that abominable powder has been scattered about I will, on my own responsibility, personally chastise the guilty student!"

He paused and looked about. Suspiciously he sniffed the air, but there was none of the powder in evidence.

"It was well for the entire class—the entire class I repeat," he said, "that there is none. Now we will proceed!"

He was unusually severe that day. The slightest slip was noticed, and the culprit was made to sit down with a lesson to write out. Scarcely one escaped, and when an error was made the professor, instead of correcting it in a gentle manner, referred sarcastically to the "imbecility" of the lad, and, in bullying language, demanded to know where he had received his early instruction.

There were murmurs of discontent. Tom flushed angrily when he was needlessly insulted, and there came a look on his face that made Jack Fitch think:

"Tom won't stand much more of this. There'll be a blow-up pretty soon, and I'll be glad of it. So will the rest of the class. Tom has something up his sleeve against Skeel, and the sooner it comes out the better. I'm going to sit tight and watch. It's time for an eruption!"

The recitation went on, from bad to worse. Student after student was rigged and browbeaten, until even those who had come to class well prepared felt their knowledge slipping from them, and they floundered, and made all sorts of wild answers and impossible guesses as to the right translation.

"It is just what I should expect of a class of cowards who would write an anonymous letter!" snarled the professor. "You must have had nice bringings-up—all of you!"

There were one or two hisses.

"Stop!" exclaimed the teacher. "I'll not permit that! I will have silence in my classes. Now, Fairfield, try again, and see if you can make any more errors than the last boy!"

Tom, with flushed face, began to recite, but he was stopped almost before he had begun.

"How many times must I tell you that your pronunciation of that word is hopelessly wrong?" snarled Professor Skeel.

"I don't believe that you ever told me so," answered Tom quietly.

"Sir!" The professor fairly glared at our hero.

Tom repeated his remark respectfully.

"That's enough!" cried the teacher. "I will not be insulted by you! Nor by any one in the class! It is evident that none of you know this lesson. You will have it again tomorrow, and, in addition twice the usual amount of Latin to do. I will hammer some knowledge into your heads in spite of yourselves!"

It was a most unfair and unjust task to inflict, and every boy resented it. Yet what could they do? All eyes seemed turned on Tom, and our hero bit his lips to keep back his temper.

"We will pass over this part of the lesson," went on the professor. "I now want you to print out for me—print out, mind, the following sentences in Latin. You will not write them, but you will print them!"

A gasp of surprise ran around the room.

CHAPTER XVI

TOM'S DARING PROPOSAL

"Silence!" proclaimed Professor Skeel, as he heard the indrawn breathing. "Not a word!"

No one seemed likely to utter it under the circumstances, but the lads were doing some hard thinking.

"As I stated, you will print this lesson," went on the instructor. "I want to see if you can print as well as you write," he added with a mocking smile.

In a flash it came to Tom and the others what the object of the queer task was. It was to gain some evidence, or clew, to the printing in the threatening letter. All eyes were turned on Tom, and then, as if aware that this might implicate him, the lads looked in various directions.

Fortunately Professor Skeel was at the board setting down the sentences he wished copied, or he might have noticed the glances turned toward our hero, and have guessed the secret. Then he would have been at no pains to try his little trick. As it was he proceeded with it, chuckling to himself as he thought that it would give him the information he desired.

But Tom was wise in his day. It was not the first time he had matched his wits against some unfair instructor, and he at once resolved on his plan.

He had printed the threatening letter in the usual, straight up and down characters. As he now began to print out the Latin exercise he used, in part, letters that sloped forward, and others that sloped backward. Not once did Tom use an upright character.

"There," he thought, as he neared the end of the short exercise, "if he thinks he can compare any of the words in this, with the words in the letter I handed him on the end of the stick, he's a good one."

Tom noticed, as did some of the others, that the words in the exercise were, in many cases, the same ones used in the letter. The professor had been enough of a detective to think of this, and he chuckled to himself many times as he thought of his cuteness. But it was not to avail him.

"You may hand in your papers as you finish," he said, "and leave the room. Don't forget—to-day's lessons, and two additional ones for to-morrow."

One by one boys filed up to his desk, laid their papers down, and passed out.

"Humph!" exclaimed Professor Skeel, as Tom passed over his exercise. "Is this your usual style of printing, Fairfield?"

"I am not used to such work, and I have no decided style. I vary it, I suppose, not having had much practice at it."

"So I see," remarked Professor Skeel, with a sharp glance at our hero—a glance that Tom returned unabashed.

"Say, what do you think of it?" asked Jack of his chum a little later, when both were in their room.

"Think of it? That it's getting worse and worse," remarked Tom bitterly. "I've had about all I can stand. Elmwood would be a perfect school, and a most jolly one, if it wasn't for Skeel."

"That's what we all think, I guess. But what's to be done?"

"Something, and that pretty soon," declared Tom with energy. "I'm not going to stand it much longer."

"Neither am I. Say, he wanted us to print that lesson so he could compare the letter with it."

"Of course. But I fooled him," and Tom told of his scheme.

"Good! I was afraid you'd be caught. We all ought to have printed part of that ultimatum, and then the responsibility would have been divided."

"Oh, I don't mind that. But if things don't turn for the better soon we'll either burn Skeel in effigy, or——"

"What?" asked Jack, as Tom paused.

"I'm not quite ready to tell yet, but it will be something rather new, I think. Now let's get at this Latin. We don't want to give him an excuse to bullyrag us any more."

"No, that's right."

While his students were working hard, and denying themselves well-earned recreation, in order to complete the unjustly imposed tasks, Professor Skeel was in his study, poring over the printed exercises turned in.

"I can't seem to identify any of the hands with the one that made up the insulting and threatening letter," he murmured, as he stared at the papers. "I thought surely Fairfield was the guilty one, and yet his printing is totally different from that in the note."

He compared the two papers—Tom's and the letter—and shook his head.

"Unless Fairfield purposely disguised his print this time!" the professor exclaimed. "I wonder if that could be it? I must get another sample from him—a natural sample. Let me see; how can I do it?" and he fell to scheming.

"There's that Bennington, too," continued the professor. "I must put the screws on him more strongly before he begins to suspect. And if I should be found out——"

The professor looked guiltily at the windows as if to make sure the shades were drawn, and, finding that they were, he listened as if fearful of hearing approaching footsteps.

He rather hoped his class would not be prepared in the unusual task he had set for them, and he was not disappointed. Few students could have prepared so much Latin in one day, with their other tasks, and many failed.

"Just as I expected!" sneered the professor. "Well, you may all remain in one hour and a half after the last lecture today, and study. Remember, the entire class remains ninety minutes after the last lecture, no matter by whom. You may go now, but return here to remain after hours."

There were gasps of dismay, for many lads had formed pleasure-plans for the afternoon. Now they could not be carried out. More than this, there were one or two students, Tom among them, who, by remaining up late the night before, and studying unusually hard, and by cutting a safe lecture, had recited perfectly. Yet they were punished with the others.

"Fellows, we've reached the limit of endurance!" exclaimed Tom to his classmates, as they filed out on the campus, and got a safe distance away from the listening ears of Professor Skeel.

"That's right!" came in a chorus.

"But what's to be done?" asked Jack.

"Hang him in effigy, and burn the scarecrow afterward!" suggested Bert Wilson.

"Can you do both?" asked George Abbot.

"Dry up, Why!" came from several.

"Let's hear from Tom," suggested Jack.

"Hear! Hear!" came the shout.

"Fellows, we've stood all we're called on to stand from Skeel," went on Tom. "I'm sick and tired of being bullyragged."

"What are we going to do?"

"Strike! Rebel!" declared Tom daringly. "I suggest that we demand better treatment from him, or we'll all go on a strike, and refuse to recite to him any more, or enter his classroom!"

"Good!"

"Great!"

"That's the stuff!"

"Hurray for Fairfield!"

"Are you in earnest, Tom?" asked Jack, who stood near his chum.

"I surely am. I've stood more from him—and so have all of us—than I would from anyone else. I say let's strike!"

"And we're with you!" came in a chorus.

"All of you?" asked Tom, looking around on the Freshman Latin class. "Remember a strike is no good unless we're all in it."

"We're all with you!" came the cry.

Tom looked around, and saw Sam Heller sneaking off.

"Here, come back, Heller!" he cried, and Sam turned, facing Tom with a sneer on his face.

CHAPTER XVII
DEFIANCE

"Well, what do you want?" demanded the bully, halting.

"I want to know where you're going," replied Tom.

"I don't know that it's any of your affair."

"Well, it is, and the affair of every member of this class. We want to know who is with us, and who against us. And it looks, the way you were sneaking off just now, as though you weren't going to be with us."

"I don't care how it looks," retorted Sam, and his tone was not as defiant as it had been, "I've got some studying to do, and I want to get at it."

"Well, we've no objection to you doing all the studying you want to," went on our hero, "but if things turn out the way I expect we won't do much more Latin boning—until things are different."

"That's what!" came in a chorus from the others.

Sam Heller started to walk away, but Tom was not done with him yet.

"Look here. Heller," went on his questioner. "What we want to know is, whether you're with us or against us?"

"Why shouldn't I be with you?"

"That's not answering the question. We know how you trained in with the Sophomores at the hazing, and that doesn't look as though you considered yourself a Freshman, though I know why you did it, all right," and Tom looked at his enemy significantly.

"That's what!" shouted Jack Fitch.

"Now, as I said," went on Tom, "if we do strike, and refuse to recite to Skeel, it won't amount to anything unless the class stands together. If even one member backs down it will look as though he didn't believe our cause right and just, and we can't afford to have that. Now, are you with us or against us? We want to know before we go any further."

"And if you're not with us, it won't be healthy for you, Heller!" exclaimed Frank Ralston.

"Hold on!" cried Tom. "We mustn't have any threats. If he doesn't want to join he doesn't have to, in which case, of course, he can no longer consider himself a Freshman in the real sense of the word."

"Coventry for his, if he doesn't join!" cried Jack.

Sam started. He knew what it would mean to be given the "silence" by every member of his class. He would be practically ignored. For, in spite of his mean traits, he had a few friends beside Nick.

"Well?" asked Tom. "What about it?"

"I—I'm with you—of course."

"To the end?"

"Yes."

"No matter what happens?"

"What do you mean?"

"I mean will you chance expulsion if it comes to that in case we strike?"

"I—I suppose so."

"That's all I want to know," went on Tom. "We will have a meeting to-night, and decide on a plan. Then we'll make a mutual promise to stick together, and we'll wait our chance. Meeting's adjourned."

"Say, Tom Fairfield is all right!" exclaimed Bert Wilson to Jack, as the two walked on together.

"That's true," agreed Tom's special chum. "I'm glad we've got him to run things."

"What makes him that way—always doing things?" George Abbot wanted to know.

"Because, Why," spoke Jack, "Tom eats rusty nails for breakfast. They give him an iron constitution."

"Really. Are you joking?"

"Of course not," replied Jack with a sober face. "Run along now, and ask Demy Miller if he knows his ancient history."

The studious janitor was observed coming over the campus, a book, as usual, under his arm. He saw the students and turned to meet them.

"What is it now, Demy?" asked Jack, as he saw an anxious look on the man's face.

"Oh, it's this proposition about constructing squares on the sides of a right-angle triangle and making the sum of them equal the one constructed on the—er—hippenuse, I think it's called."

"Hypothenuse—the hypothenuse!" laughed Jack, as he heard the odd pronunciation. "Why, that's an easy problem, Demy. George Abbot here will show you how. We're going for a skate."

"Oh, I——!" began the human question box. He was going skating also, but now he had to stop and explain to the janitor. And it was well to keep in with the latter, for he often did the boys favors, and many a night he let them in before some prowling monitor could spy them. "Well, come over here, and I'll do it for you," ended George, as he saw his chums making appealing signals to him.

Soon he was explaining that comparatively simple geometrical problem while the others, including Tom, went down to the frozen river.

Early that evening there was secret meeting of the Freshman Latin class, and a solemn agreement was entered into that, if they had to strike, they would all stick together. Even Sam Heller was present, though with no very good grace, and he made the promise with the others.

"Now to await developments," suggested Tom. "We'll give that old taskmaster one more chance, and if he takes it, and bullyrags us any more, we'll defy him, and go on strike."

"Hurray!" yelled Jack Fitch.

"That's the talk!" came from several.

"Meeting's adjourned," said Tom with a smile. "Come on, Jack, I feel just like running the guard."

"Oh, I don't know. Where you going?"

"What's the matter with going into town, and seeing a moving picture show."

"We may be nabbed."

"What of it? Might as well be killed for a sheep as a lamb. If we go into this strike business we'll get in bad with the powers that be, anyhow. And if we don't, why I'll feel so good at the change in Skeel, that I won't mind a little rigging for being out after hours."

"All right. I'm with you."

The two chums went, with some other of their friends, and thoroughly enjoyed themselves at the show, for the pictures were of a high class. Coming back the boys were almost at their dormitory, when a friendly Senior warned them that some of the proctor's scouts were on the watch.

"Go around by Skeel's house, cut through his garden, and you can get in through the cellar, I think," the Senior advised them.

"Thanks," called Tom, as he and his chums moved off in the darkness. As they passed the residence of the disliked instructor, they saw a light in his study. The shade was drawn, but the shadow of two figures could be seen on the shade. And, as the lads came opposite it they made out one figure, which plainly was that of the professor, shaking his fist at the other.

"He's laying down the law to some one," murmured Jack. "Looks like he'd be in a sweet temper to-morrow."

"I'm going to see who it is," whispered Tom. "The shade is up a crack."

"Better not," advised Bert Wilson, but Tom was daring. He crept up to the window, and saw that it was Bruce Bennington who was with the professor.

"And it was him whom the professor was shaking his fist at," thought Tom, as he stole back to his comrades with the information. "I wish I could find out what is up between those two, and what is troubling Bruce."

Our friends managed to get to their rooms without being caught, though one or two of them had narrow escapes.

Tom's thoughts, as he dropped off to sleep, were on what might happen the next day. Would it be necessary to strike? He imagined that it would, for it could hardly be expected that Professor Skeel would change his nature in a day.

It was not without a little feeling of nervousness that Tom and his associates filed into their Latin recitation the next morning. There was a grim smile on the face of Professor Skeel as he looked over the lads in their seats, and there was grim menace in the manner in which he opened his book, prepared to go on with the doubly-imposed task.

"Well," he began, omitting the usual "young gentlemen," with which jolly Professor Hammond, and the others of the faculty, used to greet their students. "Well, I trust you are all prepared; for if you are not, I warn you all that it will go hard with you."

There was a subdued murmur. Clearly there was to be no let-up in the manner of conducting the Latin class.

"Silence!" snapped Mr. Skeel. "I have had enough of this insubordination."

"You'll have more before we're through with you," thought Tom.

"You may recite, Fitch," spoke Professor Skeel. "And I want a perfect recitation from you to-day."

Jack began. He did well enough for the first few lines and then began to stumble and hesitate.

"That will do!" snapped the professor. "You try, Fairfield."

There was an indrawing of breaths. If the clash was to come, it would be with Tom, all thought.

Tom had the one day's lesson perfectly. He rapidly translated that and stopped.

"Well, go on," ordered Mr. Skeel, obviously ill-pleased that the student he suspected had done so well.

"That's as far as I'm going," said Tom quietly.

"What?"

"That's as far as I'm going. That is all that is ever assigned to us for one day."

"But I told you all to learn a double lesson."

"And I refuse to do it. We all refuse to do it!"

This was the signal Tom had agreed upon as marking the defiance and revolt, in case there was no change in the professor's manner.

For a moment Professor Skeel was dumb—as if he could not believe what he had heard.

"Will you kindly repeat that?" he asked Tom, in a quiet, menacing voice.

"I said," began our hero, "that we have agreed that the double lesson was unfair. We have agreed that if you insisted on it that we would not recite. We will go no farther. Either we get better treatment, or we will not come to your class any more."

"Wha—what?" gasped Professor Skeel, turning pale.

Tom repeated what he had said.

"What does this mean? Have done with this nonsense!"

"It means a strike!" cried Tom, turning to his classmates. "Boys, are you with me? A strike for better treatment in the Latin class! Are you with me?"

"Yes! Yes! Yes!" came the cries from all parts of the room.

"Silence! Sit down!" shouted Professor Skeel, as he saw the students rise in a body. "Sit down!" He banged his rule on the desk.

"Come on!" ordered Tom, and the boys—every one—followed his lead.

CHAPTER XVIII
THE STRIKE

For a moment amazement held Professor Skeel motionless. Several boys were filing through the door before he could manage to make a move. Then he sprang to the portal.

"Stop!" he commanded. "I demand that this nonsense cease. Return to your seats, and continue the recitation!"

"Will you hear us on just one day's lesson—the usual length?" asked Tom, turning back.

"No! Certainly not! You will do exactly as I say, and recite the double lesson. I will make no compromise."

"Then it's a strike," replied Tom. "Come on."

The boys continued to follow him. For a moment it looked as if Professor Skeel would resort to physical measures and hold the boys in his room, but he did not.

He scowled at them, but the fact that there were several large lads in the class, lads who had a reputation as boxers, probably deterred him. The last student filed out, and under the leadership of Tom they all stood in the corridor.

"Well, we did it," remarked Jack, and there was a trace of awe in his voice. It was the first time, in his experience that a class had "struck," against a disliked teacher. He was a little doubtful of the outcome.

"Of course we did it," replied Tom. "It was the only thing to do."

"And what's the next thing?" asked Bert Wilson.

"Go to history lecture, as soon as it's time," declared Tom. "We've half an hour yet. I suggest that we act quietly and as if nothing had happened. Report as usual in history class."

"But what will Skeel be doing?" inquired Jack.

"We'll have to wait and see. It's up to him now. I know one thing, though, I'll never go back to his class until he admits that he was in the wrong, and releases us from double lessons. That's what I'm going to do, and I don't care if they suspend me!"

"The same here!" came from several, and then the lads dispersed to their rooms, to do a little studying on history, or to various parts of the campus.

As for Professor Skeel, that worthy did not know what to do at first. Clearly he had been outwitted, and by Freshmen! He must recover and maintain his reputation as a disciplinarian, somehow, but how?

"I'll—I'll suspend every one of them until they beg my pardon!" he exclaimed. "As for that Fairfield, I'll see that he is expelled! The insolent puppy!"

But mere words never did any good yet, and Professor Skeel knew this. He must act, and he resolved to hit on some plan that would give him the victory. But first blood had been drawn by the students, and he realized that.

He decided to remain in his lecture room until the period was up, in order that he might think, and so that none of his fellow members on the faculty would not ask embarrassing questions as to how his class had disappeared.

"I'll get even with them," he declared. "They shall beg my pardon, and do more work than ever before."

He decided that he must first lay the matter before Doctor Meredith, for he could not act on his own initiative. He would ask that stringent measures be taken. With this in view, at the time when Tom and his chums were filing into history class, as if nothing had happened, Professor Skeel sought the head master.

There was a little feeling of nervousness on the part of our hero and his associates as they faced Professor Whitely, who had ancient history at his finger tips, but, though he had heard some rumors of trouble in the Freshman Latin class, he did not refer to it, but plunged at once into the work of the day.

Nor did anything take place during the remainder of the lectures which filled up time until about two o'clock. In the meantime, however, Professor Skeel had placed the matter before Doctor Meredith.

"They went on strike, you say?" asked the head master. "Bless my soul! I never heard of such a thing! I have known laboring bodies to refuse to work, but how can students strike?"

"By refusing to recite, or to remain in class," answered the Professor.

"And did the Freshmen do that?"

"They certainly did."

"Dear, dear! What a situation!" exclaimed Doctor Meredith. "What a peculiar position! I really never heard of one like it."

"Nor I," admitted Professor Skeel dryly. "But something must be done."

"Oh, assuredly; most assuredly," Doctor Meredith answered his colleague.

"And something drastic!" went on the Latin instructor.

"Oh, yes,—er—I suppose so. Really it is rather a novelty—a strike of students."

"Novelty!" puffed Professor Skeel.

"Yes. I never heard of such a thing. Really I think some sort of psychological study might be made of it—the causes and effects you know. What peculiar action of the brain cells brought it about. The reason for it. I think I shall write a paper on it for the International society. It will create a sensation, I think."

"I think so myself. But, in the meanwhile, something must be done—something drastic. The strike must be broken."

"Oh, of course. I—er—I perfectly agree with you," and Doctor Meredith spoke dreamily. He was already forming in his mind the chief points for a paper he determined to write on students striking. "We should have to begin with the cause," he murmured. "Ah, by the way, Professor Skeel, what was the reason the Freshmen walked out, and refused to recite?"

"They declared they would not do the lessons I had set for them."

"Why not?"

"They said they were too long—or rather, their leader, Tom Fairfield, did."

"Ah, and so they have a leader, just as in an industrial strike. Very interesting, very."

"Interesting!"

"Yes—er—that is from a psychological standpoint, of course."

"Oh, I see. But something must be done. Even though, as a punishment for careless work, I doubled the usual lesson, that is no excuse for striking."

"Oh, and so you doubled their lessons? Well, I suppose they naturally resented that. But, of course, as you say, I presume that was no excuse. But I will do something. I will act at once. I have thought of the best plan."

"What is it?" asked Professor Skeel, hoping it was the suspension of the entire class, and the expulsion of Tom.

"We will treat with the strikers, just as is done in industrial strikes," said Doctor Meredith with an air of triumph, as if he had discovered a most unusual way of settling the trouble. "We will arbitrate. That is the best way. I will send them a personal communication, when they have assembled. I must make some notes. If you will kindly post a bulletin, requesting the class to assemble in, say, the gymnasium, I will send a communication to them. That, I believe is the usual way the authorities treat with strikers. I will personally communicate with them," and with a delighted air, and a childish eagerness, Doctor Meredith took out pen and paper.

"I am to post a bulletin, calling the students together, am I?" asked Professor Skeel, not altogether relishing his work.

"Yes, and I will communicate with them. Wait, better still, I will speak to them in person."

"And what will you say?"

"I will ask them to return to your class room, and resume the interrupted session and lecture," spoke the head master with an air of triumph, as though he had made a most astounding discovery. "I will point out to them how foolish it was to strike, I will assure them that there will be no more double lessons in the future, and I will talk with them, and get at the reasons that impelled them to strike. I can use their answers in the paper I propose to write."

"Is—is that all you will do?" asked Professor Skeel, much disappointed.

"That is all that will be necessary," replied Doctor Meredith mildly. "You will see, Professor Skeel, I will soon break the strike. I think that 'break' is the proper word; is it not?"

"Yes, but it will not be broken that way, Doctor Meredith. Drastic measures are needed. Very drastic!"

"We will try my way first," decided the head master quietly. "Write out the bulletin, Professor."

CHAPTER XIX
NEGOTIATIONS END

Much against his will, and very much opposed to the mild method proposed by Doctor Meredith, Professor Skeel wrote and posted the following bulletin:

"Members of the Freshman Latin Class will assemble in the gymnasium at once, at the request of Doctor Meredith, to receive a personal communication from him.

"BURTON SKEEL."

It did not take long for it to be discovered, for some student or other was always on the alert for notices, athletic or otherwise, posted on the common bulletin board.

Bert Wilson was the first Freshman to know of it, and he darted off, post-haste, to tell Tom, who was in his room with Jack.

"I say, Tom!" exclaimed Bert. "Come on! Something doing in the strike!"

"How?"

Bert told of the notice, and soon the board was surrounded by a curious throng of students. From his window, where he was still in communication with Professor Skeel, Doctor Meredith saw the throng.

"There, you see!" he exclaimed triumphantly. "They are interested at once. They will listen to reason, surely. I wish you would come in person, and tell them that if they will recite to you the double lesson, you will impose no more."

"But I refuse to make any such agreement as that. And I don't believe they will listen to reason. Moreover, I shall have something to say to you after the meeting," snapped Professor Skeel.

"Very well. See, they are filing off to the gymnasium now. I will soon go there to speak to them."

Tom and his chums were indeed hurrying to the athletic building, and tongues were freely wagging on the way.

"What do you suppose is up?" asked George Abbot.

"Don't know," replied Jack shortly.

"Doctor Meredith is going to take a hand," commented Luke Fosdick.

"And he'll listen to reason," spoke Tom. "But, even if he requests it we're not going to knuckle down to Skeel; are we?"

"Surely not," came in a chorus.

"The strike ends when he stops imposing double lessons on us for no reason at all, but because he is ugly," went on Tom. "How about that?"

"We're with you!"

"And if he doesn't give in," proceeded our hero, "we'll——"

"Burn Skeel in effigy, after we hang him!" came the cry from some one.

"That's it," assented Tom, glad to see that his chums were with him.

They filed into the gymnasium, and the buzz of talk continued until some one announced that Doctor Meredith and Professor Skeel were approaching.

"Ah, young gentlemen, good afternoon!" greeted the head master, as he walked in and took his stand on the platform, where the secretaries and officers of the various athletic committees presided, when there was a class or school session. Professor Skeel, with a grim look in his face, followed, and sat down.

"I am informed that you are on a strike," began Doctor Meredith. "Very interesting, I'm sure—I mean of course it is altogether wrong," he added hastily. "You should have tried arbitration first. However, since you have decided to strike, I am glad to be able to speak to you—to reason with you.

"I understand that you object to having to do a double lesson as a punishment. Now I dislike to have a strike in the school, and, though I do not, for one minute, admit that you are in the right, I wish to know, if Professor Skeel agrees to give out no more double lessons, will you return to your class?"

"I will make no such agreement!" shouted the irate instructor.

"Then the strike is still on!" exclaimed Tom, springing to his feet.

"Silence!" stormed Professor Skeel.

Doctor Meredith held up his hand. The commotion that had started, at once ceased.

"I will hear what Fairfield has to say," spoke the head master, quietly.

"We have stood all we can," went on Tom. "We do not think Professor Skeel treats us fairly. We protested once, and——"

"By an anonymous letter!" broke in the Latin teacher.

"Yes, that was hardly right," commented the doctor, gently.

"It was the best way we could think of," spoke Tom. "We wanted better treatment. We want it yet, and we are going to get it, or we will continue to refuse to recite to Professor Skeel. We will continue to strike."

"Strong words," said the head master. "But may I ask how you came to hit on—er this—er—rather novel form of rebellion? I am anxious to know," and he prepared to make some notes in a book. Professor Skeel fairly snorted with rage.

"It began from the very first," explained Tom, and he went over the different steps in their trouble with the unpopular professor. "Now we can stand it no longer. We will leave school, if necessary, to gain our rights."

Doctor Meredith looked surprised at this. The loss of the Freshman Latin class would mean a serious blow to the finances of the institution of learning. Still he would have done his duty in the face of this if he saw it clearly. But he was not at all in sympathy with the methods of Professor Skeel, and the boys probably realized this.

"And so we struck," ended Tom, concluding the history of the rebellion.

"And it is my duty to end this strike," declared the head master. "I ask you to return to your recitation in Professor Skeel's room, and I—er—I have no doubt but what matters will adjust themselves."

"We will not—we feel that we cannot—return and end the strike, unless we receive some assurance that we will be treated like gentlemen, and not imposed upon in the matter of lessons," declared Tom.

"That's right!" chorused the others.

"Silence!" commanded the professor, but he was not in command now, and the lads realized it. "Then you will remain on strike?" asked Doctor Meredith, as if surprised that his request had not been complied with.

"We must, sir," replied Tom respectfully.

"Then—er—then this ends the negotiations, I presume, young gentlemen," spoke the doctor, rather sorrowfully. "I shall have to consider what further will be done."

"We're ahead—so far," commented Tom to his chums as they filed out.

"I knew it would end this way," spoke Professor Skeel to Doctor Meredith. "You will have to be firmer. You must take the most stringent measures possible."

"What would you suggest?" asked the head master, evidently at a loss. In fact he was thinking more of writing the paper on the strike than he was of ending it.

"I will tell you my plan," spoke Professor Skeel, as he followed the doctor into his study.

CHAPTER XX
PRISONERS

"Well, what do you think will be the next move?" asked Jack, as he trudged along beside his chum as they came from the gymnasium.

"I don't know, I'm sure. It's up to them now, and we can only saw wood, and see what happens."

"Do you think they'll punish us?" asked George Abbot.

"Oh, there you go again!" cried Bert Wilson. "Can't you do anything but ask questions, Why?"

"Of course I can, but I want to know what's going to happen to us."

"There can't much more happen than has happened already," said Lew Bentfield, grimly.

"That's right," agreed Tom.

"They will probably suspend us until we give in," come from Jack.

"What of it?" asked Tom.

"Nothing, only if we're suspended we can't go to any lectures or recitations, and we'll fall behind in our work, and be conditioned when this thing is over. That means we may lose a year."

"Nonsense!" exclaimed Tom. "Besides, we agreed to stick this thing out."

"Oh, I'm not going to back out!" cried Jack quickly. "Don't imagine that for a second. Only this is a serious matter."

"I know it," admitted Tom, quietly. "And it's a serious matter to be treated as we have been treated in class nearly every day by Professor Skeel. I'm tired of being bullyragged. This strike is for principle, not for any material advantage.

"But, anyhow, if they do suspend us it can't last for long. Why, nearly every Freshman is in with us. That is, all but those who don't like Latin, and they're mighty scarce.

"Now practically the whole Freshman class of a college can't be suspended for any great length of time, and the ban will soon be raised."

"You mean we'll win?" asked Bert Wilson.

"Of course we will!" declared Tom stoutly, "and the lessons we miss, if we are suspended, we can easily make up. But I don't believe Merry will suspend us."

There were various opinions about this, and the talk became general as the boys separated, going their different ways. Tom and a group of his particular chums went to his room.

"We ought to do something to celebrate this strike," declared Jack, when there was a lull in the talk.

"That's right!" cried Tom. "I'm for something to eat. I'm going to give a little dinner here to as many as we can crowd in. Let's get busy, Jack."

"A spread!" cried Tom's chum. "Where are the eats to come from?"

"Oh, I'll sneak out and get 'em as soon as it's dark enough. You can work it so as to get some stuff from our worthy matron; can't you?"

"I guess so."

"Then leave the rest to me, and ask as many fellows of our particular crowd as you can squeeze into the room. Pack 'em in like sardines. The more the merrier. We'll make this a record spread."

"Jove, a spread just after you've organized a strike!" exclaimed Bert Wilson, admiringly. "Say, you do do things, Tom Fairfield."

"Oh, what's the use sitting around like a bump on a log?" asked our hero. "Now we'll go to supper, and mind, every fellow is to stow away in his pockets anything not in a liquid form that he can. Bring it to the feast, for I can't lug in any too much all by my lonesome."

"I'll go with you," volunteered several eagerly.

"No, if two of us go out together it will create suspicions, and all eyes are on us now, as Napoleon said to his soldiers in Egypt, or was it in South Africa? Anyhow, I'll sneak out as soon as it's dark enough, and get what I can."

There was a subdued air of expectancy at the Freshman supper that night, and many whispers ran around. It was noticed, too, that many of the lads had unusually large appetites, but they did not seem to be eating as much as they asked for. There were sly motions which some of the waiters could not understand, for they were caused when the diners slipped food into their pockets.

"Assemble in my room one at a time, as soon after the signal 'lights out' as possible," explained Tom, when the meal was over. It was a rule that the boys must have their rooms in darkness after 9:30 o'clock, unless special permission for studying was obtained. "Don't go in bunches," advised our hero, "but a few at a time. I'm off to town."

Watching his chance, Tom managed to elude a monitor, though, truth to tell, so amazing had the strike seemed to all the college authorities, that they were dazed, and really did not keep as close a watch over the Freshmen as usual.

Tom was in town, buying a lot of indigestible, but toothsome, dainties, dear to the palates of himself and his chums, when most unexpectedly, he met Bruce Bennington coming out of a pawnshop.

"Why, Bennington!" exclaimed Tom. "Oh, how are you?" and he quickly tried to change his first astonished tone, which had said, as plainly as anything: "What are you doing in such a place?"

"Oh, hello, Fairfield," greeted the Senior, after a first start of surprise. Then, in a cool voice, he added: "I suppose it looks rather odd, to see me coming out of this place, but the truth of the matter is——"

"Not at all!" interrupted Tom, determined to make amends for his seeming surprise. "I've done the same thing when I'm temporarily embarrassed. Besides, for all I know you may have been making a psychological study of the pawnbroker, eh?"

"Oh, of course," laughed Bruce uneasily. "But say, youngster, you fellows are making names for yourselves. Jove! We Freshmen never went on a strike. You've got us beaten a mile, even if we did drive a cow up on Merry's doorstep. But a strike! Never!"

"Maybe you hadn't any need," spoke Tom. "Was Skeel as bad in your time as he is now?"

"Worse, if anything. And he's a——" Bruce hesitated. "Well, I'll not say it," he concluded. "What's up, anyhow?"

"Oh, I'm going to give a little spread."

"Oh, I say now! That's adding insult to injury, as the Irishman said when the parrot called him names after biting him. You Freshies are laying it on rather thick."

"Might as well get all we can while it's coming our way," explained Tom. "No telling what may happen to-morrow."

"No, that's so. Well, I wish I was a Freshman again," and, with something like a sigh of regret, the Senior passed on.

"There's something wrong with him," mused Tom, as he caught a car that would take him near the school. "And I wonder why, with all the money he is supposed to have, that he had to go to a pawn shop? Why didn't he come to me, or some of the college boys? Too proud, I guess."

There was snow on the ground and the weather, though cold, bore a promise of more as Tom cautiously made his way by a roundabout course over the campus and to a side door.

"Well, you're all here, I see," he remarked as he entered his room, and saw a crowd of congenial lads assembled there. The door communicating with the apartment of Bert Wilson, which portal was seldom unlocked, had been opened, making a fairly large apartment in which to have a forbidden spread.

"Make out all right?" asked Jack.

"Sure, I've got a choice assortment of grub. Let's set the beds," for they were to serve as tables, covered with large squares of newspapers for table cloths.

"I've got the windows and keyholes covered," explained Jack, pointing to blankets tacked over the glass.

"Good! Now let the merry feast go on, and joy be loosed. For we'll eat to-day and starve to-morrow."

"Starve to-morrow?" gasped George Abbot. "What do you mean, Tom?"

"Nothing. I was just getting poetical, that's all. You needn't stare at the sandwiches and olives, George, my boy; they are substantial, if my poetry isn't, and they won't disappear. Come on, fellows, get busy."

The feast was soon under way, and though the boys could have had nearly everything displayed on the "bed" at their regular meal, they all agreed that the viands tasted ever so much better served in the forbidden manner that they were.

"Pass those pickles, Jed, my boy!" commanded Tom to a lanky Freshman.

"And keep that mustard moving," ordered Jack. "Those frankfurters are prime, Tom."

"I thought you'd like 'em," remarked our hero.

"Put some more on to cook," pleaded Jack.

"Sure," assented Bert Wilson, who presided at the "stove."

This was an arrangement of wires, ingeniously made by Tom, so that it fitted over the gas, and on which a saucepan could be set over the flame. In this pan the sausages were simmering.

Bert put in some more, and stood anxiously watching them, fork in hand, while George buttered rolls, and passed them around.

"I propose a toast!" exclaimed Frank Carter, rising, a bottle of ginger ale in one hand, and a big piece of chocolate cake in the other.

"Hush! Not so loud!" cautioned Jack.

"Well, then, a silent toast to our host, Tom Fairfield!" went on Frank.

"Tiger!" whispered Jack, waving his Frankfurter fork in the air.

"Thanks, one and all," replied Tom, bowing. "I will——"

"Hark!" suddenly cautioned Jack.

The boys were silent on the instant.

"I hear footsteps," whispered Bert.

There was no doubt but that some one was out in the corridor, but as silence replaced the rather noiseless celebration of the feast, the footsteps could be heard retreating.

"A spy sent to make a report," was Tom's opinion. "Well, we can't be any worse off than we are. Keep things going, fellows," and the spread proceeded.

Meanwhile a curious scene was being enacted in the study of Doctor Meredith. All the members of the faculty were present, and were being addressed by Professor Skeel.

"I think it is due me, as an instructor in this school, that this class be punished," he said.

"According to your own account they have been already—with extra lessons," remarked jolly Professor Hammond.

"That was for other breaches of discipline," declared Professor Skeel. "They have not been adequately punished for sending me the anonymous letter, nor for this strike. I think an example should be made of them."

"Well, perhaps something should be done," admitted Professor Hammond. "But I should favor a mild lesson, and then—a change of programme for the future."

"And I demand a severe lesson, and a firm hand in the future!" insisted Professor Skeel. "Unless the Freshmen are punished I shall at once resign, and the punishment I demand is the plan I first mentioned. Is it to be done, Doctor Meredith?"

"Ah—er—ahem!" stammered the mild head master. "I dislike exceedingly to take such a step, but, I suppose something should be done."

"It must be done!" demanded Professor Skeel.

"Very well then," sighed Doctor Meredith. "But it is a very strange state of affairs. However," he added more brightly, "I will have some additional matter for my paper on a strike in school," and he seemed quite delighted.

The faculty meeting broke up. So, too, in due time did the feast in Tom's room. The boys sneaked to their respective apartments. And, rather strange to say, none of them was detected. But they did not know that a special order had come from the head master to Monitor Blackford, in charge of Opus Manor.

"Humph! It was all too easy," said Jack, as he and Tom were ready to turn in at nearly midnight.

"What was?"

"This spread. Aside from that sneaking footstep we heard we were not disturbed once. I'm afraid it's the calm before the storm. And it may be a bad one. But we'll weather it."

"Of course we will," declared Jack. "Say, talk about a storm," he added, as he peered from the window, from which the blanket had been removed, "it's snowing to beat the band."

"Good," answered Tom. "We can get up a sleighing party to-morrow, if we can't go to Latin class."

When the Freshmen filed down to breakfast the next morning there was a look of surprise on every face as they glanced at the table. For at each place was a glass of water, and on each plate two slices of bread.

"What's this?"

"Is it April Fool?"

"Who thought of this joke?"

These were only a few of the remarks and questions.

"I say!" called Tom to Mr. Blackford, who came into the room, a quizzical look on his face. "Where is our breakfast?"

"On the table."

"Is that all?"

"That's all. Orders from Doctor Meredith."

"Oh, I see. He's trying to starve us into submission. I'll not stand for that!" cried Tom. "Fellows, come on!" he added. "We'll go to town to a restaurant!"

He moved to the front door.

"You can't go out, Mr. Fairfield," said the monitor firmly.

"Why not, I'd like to know."

"Because you, and all the others, in fact all the Freshmen in this dormitory, are prisoners!"

"Prisoners!" cried a score of voices.

"That's it," went on Mr. Blackford. "You are to stay locked in this building, on a diet of bread and water, until you give in!"

CHAPTER XXI
THE ESCAPE

Surprise, for a moment, held the boys dumb, and then a storm of protests broke out.

"We'll not stand it!"

"Let's raid the pantry!"

"They're trying to starve us into submission!"

"It's a relic of the dark ages, boys!" cried Bert Wilson. "A prison diet of bread and water."

"Let's break out, and go over to the Seniors' place in Elmwood Hall!" suggested Jack. "They'll feed us."

"That's right!" cried several.

"Hold on, fellows," called Tom.

At the sound of his calm voice the rush that had begun toward the door of the dining room, was halted. A look of relief came over the face of Monitor Blackford.

"Fellows!" said Tom, "this thing has come to a crisis. They're trying to break this strike by unfair means. I've no doubt that the suggestion came from Skeel. Doctor Meredith never would have done it of his own accord. Skeel has a bad influence over him. Now then, it's up to us to beat 'em at their own game!"

"But we can't live on bread and water!" declared Ned Wilton. "At least I won't. I'm not used to such fare. I always want fruit in the morning, and eggs."

"So do lots of us," said Tom quietly. "But we're not going to get it this morning, at least. Now then, let's look at this thing quietly. Let's accept it. It can't last forever. Sooner or later the story will get out, and the college faculty will have to give in. Our cause is right, and we'll win. All we ask is civil treatment, as the old sailor said after the whale chase, and blamed little of that. Here's for a hearty breakfast of bread and water."

He made a move toward his place.

"But there's not even butter on the bread!" cried Jack.

"Prisoners aren't usually furnished with luxuries," commented Tom, quietly.

"Oh, say, I'm not going to stand for this!" burst out Bert Wilson. "I'm going to leave, and wire home for permission to resign from Elmwood Hall."

He strode toward the front door, intending to see if he could get out, but Mr. Blackford stood on guard, and he was not a small man.

"It's no use, Mr. Wilson," said the monitor, quietly. "The door is locked, and you can't go out unless you break out. And it's a very strong door," he added, significantly.

With a gesture of impatience Bert turned toward a window. To his surprise he noted that the usual fastenings had been replaced by new ones, and, in addition, the casements were screwed down. Then, to the astonishment of the boys, who had not noticed it before, they became aware that bars of wood had been screwed in place across the outside of the frames.

"By Jove! They have us boxed in, all right!" cried Tom, as his attention was called to the precautions taken to keep the lads in Opus Manor. "This is what they were doing last night when we were having our fun. I've no doubt but that the spy came into the hall to see if we were likely to stay up there eating, while they got in their fine work. Oh, but we were chumps not to think of this!"

"No one would," said Jack Fitch. "I say, though, I believe if we all go together we can break out. We can handle Blackford!"

Tom shook his head. He did not intend to submit quietly, but he knew better than to act before he had a good plan.

At that moment several of the men monitors from the other dormitories were seen in the lower hall, and one or two were at a rear door.

"They're prepared to meet force with force," said Tom to his chums. "Just wait a bit, and there may be something doing. Meanwhile, eat your grub."

"Hot grub this!" exclaimed Jack. "I wish we'd saved some from last night. Any left, Tom?"

"Not a crumb. Never mind, this is good for a change," and Tom proceeded to munch the dry bread, and sip the water.

Monitor Blackford's face showed relief. He had been prepared to carry out the orders of the faculty with force, if necessary, but he rather hoped he would not have to do so, for he knew how lads can fight when they want to. Still he was glad they had submitted quietly. And he was not altogether on the side of the faculty, either.

"I guess it won't be for long, young gentlemen," he said, as he passed around the table. "I'm sure I'm very sorry to have to do it, but I'm a poor man, and my living——"

"That's all right," interrupted Tom good-naturedly. "We're not blaming you. And, as you say, it won't be for long."

"Then you're going to give in?" asked the monitor eagerly.

"Not much!" exclaimed Tom. "The faculty is, and we'll make Skeel beg our pardons. Then we'll have a roast turkey feast on Merry."

"I'm afraid you never will," spoke the monitor. "The professor is very determined. I expect he'll be over before long."

"We'll be ready for him," said Tom grimly.

Once they had made up their minds to accept the situation the boys made merry over the meager breakfast.

"Anyhow, we can cut all lectures!" exulted several who were not fond of study.

"And we'll have to pull our belts in a few holes if this sort of grub keeps up long," commented Jack.

"Yes, a fine sort of strike this is!" sneered Sam Heller. "I never agreed to starve, Tom Fairfield." He glared at his rival.

"You can starve with the rest of us," spoke our hero, grimly. "Besides, you can live a long time on bread and water. I forget the exact figures, but I think it is something over a month."

"A month!" cried Jack. "I'll never last that long."

"Neither will the strike," answered Tom, coolly. "I have something up my sleeve."

"What is it?" clamored half a dozen.

"I'll tell you later. Now to get what amusement we can. Come on up to my room, and we'll talk it over."

They did talk it over, from all standpoints, but they could not agree on what was best to be done. It was a cold, blowy, blustery day outside, the storm being not far short of a blizzard.

The dormitory was warm, but soon the healthy appetites of the lads asserted themselves, and they felt the lack of their usual good breakfast. Still, save for Sam Heller, no one thought of giving in. All stuck by Tom.

During the morning, groups of students from other dormitories, the Senior, Junior and Sophomore, came past Opus Manor, and cruelly made signs of eating, for of course the story of the imprisonment of the Freshman class was known all through the college.

"Say, I've got an idea!" exclaimed Jack, as he saw some of his friends in the upper classes standing under his window in an angle of the building. "Why can't they smuggle us something to eat? We can let down a basket or a box, and haul it up."

"That's the stuff!" cried Bert Wilson. "Let's drop 'em a note."

One was written and tossed out to Bruce Bennington and some friendly Seniors. They nodded assent as they read it, and hurried off.

"Now to make a basket of some sort!" exclaimed Jack.

"Take our fishing creels," suggested Tom, who seemed to be busily engaged in thinking out something. Accordingly the fishing baskets were tied to strings, which the boys collected from many pockets, and were made ready to be lowered for food.

In due time, under cover of the storm, which had grown so bad that the swirling flakes hid objects ten feet away, the Seniors returned with food which they had somehow obtained. There were also bottles of cold coffee and soft drinks.

"This is great!" cried Jack, as he hauled up the creels, several times, well laden. "There isn't going to be a feast, but it's something."

"And it has given me the idea I wanted!" cried Tom.

"What is it?" demanded several.

"We'll escape from the second story windows to-night! We can make ropes of the bed clothes, in real story-book fashion, lower ourselves down, and hie into town. We'll put up at some hotel or boarding houses there, and the school can get along without us until they recognize our rights."

"Good!" came in an enthusiastic chorus. "Let's start right away," added Jack.

"No, not until after dark," advised Tom. "We will be caught if we go before."

The sandwiches and other things which the Seniors had provided made a welcome addition to the slim dinner. Professor Skeel came in as the boys were about to arise from the table, probably to gloat over them. He was received with a storm of hisses.

"Stop that, instantly!" he cried, his face pale with anger.

"Keep it up," ordered Tom, and keep it up the boys did, until the discomfited instructor had to withdraw, vowing vengeance on the lads whom even a diet of bread and water, and the humiliation of being made prisoners, could not subdue.

"But I'll break their spirit yet!" said the professor, grimly.

The preparations for the escape went on. Several ropes were made from torn sheets and light blankets, and fastened to heavy objects as anchors, in various room whence the lads were to take French leave. Several were to drop from Tom's window.

The storm grew worse, and the boys put on their heaviest garments. Night approached, the bread and water supper was served, and Mr. Blackford remarked to his wife:

"I don't see what makes the boys so cheerful."

"Maybe they are up to some mischief," she suggested.

"How could they be?" he asked. "They can't get out to get anything to eat, for the doors and windows are all fastened."

"Well, you never can tell what boys are going to do," she said. "I'd be on the watch."

"I will," agreed her husband, and he and the other monitors looked well to the fastening of the doors and casements.

"All ready now, boys?" asked Tom, as it grew darker.

"All ready," answered Jack. "I don't believe they can see us now."

"Go easy," advised Tom. "Hold on tight going down, and don't slip. One at a time, and we'll meet at the twin oaks on the far edge of the campus, and tramp into town. The car line is blocked, I guess, with all this snow."

One by one the boys slid down the improvised ropes, going from rooms where they could drop to the ground unobserved from any of the lower windows.

"Are we all here?" asked Tom, when the escape was finally concluded, and the crowd of students had assembled under the oak trees, the few brown leaves of which rustled in the wintry blast.

"I guess so," answered Jack. "But I didn't see Sam Heller."

"I saw him slide down a rope from Pete Black's room," remarked Bert Wilson, "and then I noticed that he sneaked off by himself."

"Let him go," suggested Tom. "We're better off without him."

"Unless he's going to squeal on us," came from Jack, suddenly.

CHAPTER XXII
THE BURNING EFFIGY

"That's so!" exclaimed Tom, after a moment's consideration. "I never thought of that. It would be just like Sam. Oh, but what's the use worrying, anyhow? They'll know, sooner or later, that we've escaped, and anything that sneak Heller can tell them won't do us any harm. Come on to town."

They headed into the storm, which seemed to become worse every minute, with the wind whipping the stinging flakes into the faces of the lads, who bent to the blast.

"I say!" cried Horace Gerth. "This is fierce!"

"The worst ever!" cried Jack.

"You can turn back, if you want to," commented Tom, grimly. "Back to bread and water."

"Not for mine!" exclaimed Bert Wilson.

"Me for a hot meal in town," declared Tom. "I'll stand treat if any fellows are short of cash."

"Good!" cried several, as they trudged on.

It did not take very long to make the lads aware that they were in for a bad time. The snow was drifted heavily and the road to town, never good at the best, was almost impassable. As Tom had predicted, the trolley cars had long since ceased running, and there was not a vehicle track to be seen in the darkness, that was but faintly relieved by the white snow.

"We're going to have a hard pull of it," commented Jack, as he floundered to Tom's side.

"That's right. I wish we had had a better night for the escape, but we had to take our chance."

"Oh, of course. But it will be all right when we strike the town, and get some hot coffee. How far is it, anyhow?"

"Oh, about two miles, I guess."

"Two miles of this!" groaned Jack, as he bent his head to a particularly fierce blast. "It's heavy going."

On and on the boys floundered. The first enthusiasm was wearing off, and they became aware of the stinging cold and the fierce wind that cut through even the heaviest coats. But they did not think of giving up.

After an hour of tramping, during which the storm seemed to be doing its best to drive the boys back, and during which time several began to murmur discontentedly, Jack suddenly exclaimed:

"I say, Tom, do you think we're on the right road?"

"I don't know. What do you think?"

A halt was called.

"I can't make out anything," declared Jack. "It's as dark as a pocket, and, even in day time, with this storm, we couldn't see very far. My private opinion is that we are lost."

"Lost!"

"Yes, that is, not seriously lost," went on Tom, with a trace of jollity in his voice, "but just lost enough so that we can't strike town to-night."

"Then what are we going to do?" asked George Abbot.

"There you go again—the eternal question!" complained Jack. "We'll have to go back, that's all, I guess."

"I don't like to," said Tom. "Let's have another try for the road. That row of trees over there looks like it." He pointed to a row dimly visible through the storm.

"Well, come on, one more try," assented Jack, and though there was some grumbling, none of Tom's followers deserted him.

On they floundered through the snow, only to find, when they go to the trees, that they were on the edge of a gully.

"But I know where we are, at any rate," declared Bert. "I believe I can find our way back to school from here, even if I can't lead you to town."

"All right, then do it," assented Tom wearily, for he was tired, and rather chagrined at the failure of his plan. "But, one thing, fellows, if we do go back we've got to make a showing."

"How?" asked several voices.

"We'll burn Skeel in effigy before we go in, and then they can do as they like to us."

"Hurray!"

"That's what!"

"We'll have a demonstration," went on Tom, "and the whole school will come out. We'll take advantage of it to ask the fellows to contribute something to our support. We'll get more food and then—well, we'll see what happens in the morning."

"We're with you!" cried his chums.

They turned back, hardly any but what were glad to get the wind and stinging flakes out of their faces, and, led by Bert, they were soon on familiar ground.

"There's Elmwood Hall," said Jack to Tom, as they tramped on together through the storm, when a dull mass loomed up before them. "What's the programme?"

"First to make the effigy."

"How you going to do it?"

"Oh, I've had it planned for several days. In the barn I've got some old clothes hidden, and a hat just like Skeel wears. All we've got to do is to stuff the coat and pants with straw, tie a rope to it, hoist it on the flag pole halyards and set fire to it. Then things will happen of themselves."

"I guess they will!" exclaimed Jack, admiringly.

It was quiet around the college when the Freshmen came back after their partly unsuccessful escape. That their going had been discovered no one doubted, but there seemed to be no one on the watch for them, and no undue excitement in Opus Manor.

"Now for the effigy!" exclaimed Tom, as he told the others his plans. "Jack and I, and a few of us are enough. The rest of you stand ready to give our yell as the fire starts."

It did not take long, in the barn, and with the light of several lanterns which Tom had hidden, to make the effigy of Professor Skeel. It did not look much like him, but the hat added the necessary identification.

None of the school employees was about the stable, and the boys had easy sailing.

"Now to string it up, and set fire to it!" cried Tom.

"How you going to burn it when it's up in the air?" asked Bert.

"I'll make a sort of fuse of twisted straw that will hang down, and I can touch that off from the ground," was the answer.

With their mates crowding around them, Tom and his chums brought out the effigy. A rope had been provided by our hero, who seemed to think of everything, and soon it was attached to the flag halyards and the image was mounting the pole through the blinding storm and darkness.

"Here we go!" cried Tom, as, with some difficulty he struck a match and set the straw fuse ablaze. "Now for the yell!"

It was given with a will as the fire slowly enveloped the effigy, and, in response, there was a rush from the dormitories of the various classes, for it was not late yet.

"Three hisses for Professor Skeel!" called someone, and it sounded as if a den of snakes had been loosed.

Brighter and brighter grew the flames. The effigy was shown in bold relief. All the college seemed pouring out, heedless of the storm.

A figure came running over the snow. A voice called out—a harsh voice:

"I demand that this outrage cease at once!"

It was Professor Skeel himself.

CHAPTER XXIII
TOM'S FIND

For a moment the Freshmen paused in their wild dancing about the pole, from which hung suspended the burning effigy. And then, as they saw the indignant figure of the disliked professor, and as they heard his demand, they broke out into a further storm of hisses that sounded above the blast of the wintry wind.

"Stop it! Stop it at once! Take down that disgraceful image!" demanded Professor Skeel. In spite of the crude way in which it had been made he—and others as well—could easily recognize that it was intended for him, by the hat. "Take it down!" he shouted.

"Never!" came the defiant cry from the Freshmen. They were not so cold now, but they were hungry and tired, and they saw in Professor Skeel the individual who, they believed, was responsible for their troubles.

"Three hisses for the professor!" called someone, and again they were given with vigor.

"Take it down! Take it down!" fairly screamed the enraged instructor. He looked around. The whole school was witnessing the spectacle of disgrace that had been arranged for his benefit. Every student was present, arranged in a big circle about the jubilant Freshmen, and most of the faculty had come to the doors of their residences to look on.

"I demand that this outrage cease at once!" cried Professor Skeel, but no move was made to heed his request. In fact, the Freshman only cheered themselves, and hissed him the louder.

Professor Skeel could stand no more. With glaring eyes he made a rush for the crowd of students, darting through the storm that still raged.

"Look out! Here he comes!" warned Jack to Tom.

"All right. I'm ready for him," was the quiet answer. "But I don't believe he'll do anything more than try to pull down the image."

"Will you let him?"

"I think not. Still I don't want to get into a personal encounter with a teacher. Let's form a ring around the pole, and prevent him from touching the ropes. The effigy will soon be burned out, anyhow." The flames were eating the image slowly, as the cloth and straw was moist, and the snow flakes further dampened them.

"That's a good idea!" commented Jack. "Hi, fellows, no surrender. We must protect our effigy!"

"That's what!" came the rallying chorus, and under Tom's direction the lads formed a cordon about the pole.

Professor Skeel was speeding through the drifts. He reached the nearest lads, and roughly thrust them aside. Tom had quickly whispered to those nearest the pole not to fight back, but to offer passive resistance. So, too, those on the outer edge did not make any hostile movement when the irate instructor went through them with a rush.

"Get away from that pole! Let me take that disgraceful image down! I shall insist upon the most severe punishment to every one concerned in this outrage!" stormed Professor Skeel.

"Stick to your posts!" cried Tom.

"As for you, Fairfield!" shouted the professor. "This will be your last appearance here! You incited the students to do this!"

"Correct guess!" whispered Jack with a grin.

Professor Skeel did not find it as easy as he had thought, to thrust the lads away from the pole, so that he might loose the ropes. As fast as he shoved one lad aside, in which operation no active resistance was offered, another Freshman took his place, and there was a constant shifting and whirling mass of students about the pole. It was utterly impossible for the professor to get to the ropes.

"This must stop! It shall stop!" he cried. "I—I shall be under the necessity of personally chastising you if you do not at once remove the image!" he added.

"Stick, boys!" sung out Tom.

"Then take the consequences," shouted the instructor. He struck one of the smaller lads, who drew back his fist. In another moment there would have been presented the not very edifying sight of an encounter between teacher and pupil.

But Professor Skeel found himself suddenly clasped from behind, while Tom, worming his way to the side of the lad who had been hit, caught his upraised arm.

"It's all right, Henry," he called in his ear. "It's all over I guess. Hammond has hold of Skeel."

This was true. The big fat, jolly professor, seeing how matters were likely to turn out, had made his way into the throng, and had seized his colleague.

"You had better come with me," he advised, quietly. "You are forgetting yourself, Professor Skeel. You can do no good here. The boys are past reasoning with."

"I shall not go until they have taken down that disgraceful effigy of me."

"It will soon burn down. Besides, Doctor Meredith is coming out to speak to them. I have sent for him. You had better come with me."

Much against his will, Professor Skeel allowed himself to be led away. The boys had stopped hissing and cheering now, for they saw that the crisis had come, and that they were either to win their strike, or that some unusual measures would be taken.

"Here comes Merry!" exclaimed Jack in a hoarse whisper, as he descried the form of the venerable head of the school making his way through the storm. The burning effigy still gave light enough to see, reflected as it was by the snow on the ground and the swirling flakes in the air.

Professor Skeel left with Professor Hammond, and, as they passed the outer ring of Freshman, there came a cry:

"Three cheers for Professor Hammond!"

They were given with the "Tiger!" at the end.

Doctor Meredith made his way to where he could command a view of the class that had revolted.

"Young gentlemen!" he began in a mild voice.

"Three cheers for the Doctor!" were called for and given.

"Young gentlemen," he went on, with a benevolent smile, "you will kindly cease this demonstration, and return to your dormitory."

"Does that mean we win?" asked Tom respectfully. "We went on strike for better treatment in the Latin class. If we go back, and call the strike off, do we get it?"

"That's what we want to know," added Jack Fitch.

"And we want something to eat, too," spoke Bert Wilson.

"You will return to your dormitory," went on Doctor Meredith in an even voice. "This must go on no longer."

"But what about the Latin class?" asked Tom persistently. "Are we to be prisoners? Aren't we to be allowed to recite, or attend lectures?"

"I will settle all that tomorrow," said the doctor. "I may state, however, that you will recite, if you do at all to-morrow, to another Latin instructor."

"Hurray! That's what we want to know!" yelled Tom. "Come on, boys!" he added. "Back to bed. The strike is over!"

"I don't see how," said Jack. "He hasn't said that Skeel will be any different."

"Aw, can't you see through a hole in a millstone?" asked Tom. "Can't you see that Skeel isn't going to be our teacher any more?"

"What do you mean?"

"I mean that there's going to be a shift. No more of Skeel's Latin for us. The doctor has seen that it won't do, and he's put his foot down. Skeel can't dictate to him any more. The strike is over—we've won, and it will be admitted to-morrow. Come on to bed."

"But about the eats?" suggested Bert. "I'm half starved. What about the eats?"

"Young gentlemen!" spoke Doctor Meredith again.

Instantly there was silence.

"Young gentlemen, you will return to your dormitory. But you may first stop in the dining hall."

"For bread and water?" asked some one.

"For—er—for your usual hot supper," said the doctor, with a smile.

"Hurray!" yelled Tom. "The strike is sure over! We win!"

The last flickering embers of the burning effigy died out and the scene was almost dark. Doctor Meredith returned to his house. The other students turned back into their dormitories. The Freshmen made a break from around the flag staff and ran toward the place where a much-needed supper awaited them.

As Tom, with Jack at his side, hurried across the spot where Professor Skeel had struck the Freshman, our hero saw something black lying on the snow. He stopped and picked it up.

"Someone's pocketbook," he remarked. "I'll look inside for a name, and return it. Oh, Jack, we win!"

"And we're going to eat!" added Jack with a sigh of satisfaction. As they entered the dining hall they saw Sam Heller there. He had sneaked back when the others were escaping and had practically surrendered. He was hissed when this became known.

CHAPTER XXIV

THE SAVING OF BRUCE

"What have you there, Tom?" asked Jack. They were in their room, some time after the riot over the burning effigy, and following a more bountiful supper than they had partaken of in many a long day. They had talked over the events and Sam Heller's desertion.

"Oh, but you should see those boys eat!" exclaimed Mrs. Blackford to her husband, after a visit to the dining hall.

"I don't blame them," was the answer. "I'm glad it's over, and that they have won. I never did like that Skeel." The monitor had confided to Tom that as soon as Doctor Meredith had word of the return of the students from their unsuccessful trip toward the town, he had ordered a big supper gotten ready. And now Tom and his chum were in their room, tired but happy.

"This," remarked Tom, as he looked at the object to which Jack referred, "this is a pocketbook I picked up out on the campus near the flag pole. Some one dropped it during the excitement, I guess. I'll see if there's a name in it, so I can send it back."

He opened it. There were some banknotes and a number of papers. Tom rapidly looked the latter over, and, as he caught sight of one, he uttered a whistle of amazement.

"What's the matter?" asked Jack, who was getting ready for bed. "Whose wallet is it?"

"Professor Skeel's."

"Nothing remarkable in that; is there?"

"No, but it's what I found in it. Now I know why he has such a hold over Bruce, and what that lad's trouble is. Look here, Jack," and the two boys bent their heads over a slip of paper.

"I should say so!" exclaimed Jack. "No wonder he looked troubled, and acted it, too. What are you going to do about it?"

"I'm going to save Bruce; that's what I'm going to do."

"How?"

"I don't just know yet, but I'll find a way."

There was subdued excitement the next morning when the Freshmen filed down to breakfast, and the talk was of nothing but the uprising of the night before. Sam Heller was practically ignored, but he did not seem to mind.

"Are we to get bread and water this morning, Blackie?" asked Tom, of the monitor, at the same time playfully poking him in the ribs.

"No, sir, the usual meal."

"And are we still locked in?" demanded Jack.

"No, sir, you can go wherever you like. Chapel I should imagine, first."

"Oh, of course," agreed Tom. "I want my eggs soft boiled," he added most prosaically.

On the way to the morning devotions Tom pulled out the wallet.

"I guess I'll send this over to Skeel's house, instead of taking it myself," he said to Jack. "It might raise a row if I went there." And, requesting one of the assistant janitors to do the errand, Tom proceeded to chapel. Thus the wallet was returned to its owner, but minus a certain bit of paper.

"Well, you fellows certainly cut things loose!" exclaimed Bruce Bennington admiringly to Tom, as he met our hero later. "You won hands down. I wish I could do things as easily as you seem to do," and he sighed. Tom noticed that the look of worry and trouble on the Senior's face was deepened.

"Look here, Bruce!" exclaimed Tom. "I wish you would tell me exactly what your trouble is. Maybe I can help you."

"No you couldn't."

"I think so," and there was a peculiar note in Tom's voice. "Tell me," he urged. The two were walking by themselves over a deserted part of the snow-covered campus. The storm had ceased, and the day, though clear, was quite cold. The weather was crisp and fine.

"Hanged if I don't tell you!" burst out Bruce. "I don't know why it is, but I took a liking to you the first time I saw you. I had half a notion to tell you then, but I didn't. I haven't told anyone—I wish, now, I had. Now I'm going to tell you. It's come to a show-down, anyhow. I was just on my way to see Professor Skeel. He's at the bottom of my trouble, as you may have guessed. He has sent for me. The jig is up."

"I'll go with you," volunteered Tom. "I fancy I know part of your trouble, at least."

"You do?" burst out Bruce in amazement.

"Yes. Look at that," and Tom held out a bit of paper.

"I say, Tom," hailed Jack from a distance, as he came running up. "What are we to do? There's a notice posted, saying we are to go to Latin recitation to Professor Hammond, temporarily, and then afterward the Freshmen are to meet Doctor Meredith and Professor Skeel. That looks as if we hadn't won after all. The boys are anxious."

"I'll be with them in a little while," answered Tom. "It's all right. We win the strike all right, only things have to be adjusted formally I suppose. But I'll say this. I'll never apologize to Skeel, and he's got to promise to be decent, or the strike will begin all over again."

"Hurray! That's the stuff!" cried Jack. "That's what we want to know. But aren't you coming to the lecture?"

"In a little while—yes. I've got something else on hand now, Jack."

"All right!" called his chum, knowingly. "I'm on. See you later," and he ran off. Jack turned to Bruce.

Over the face of the Senior had come a curious change. His trouble seemed to have vanished.

"Tom—Tom Fairfield!" he exclaimed. "You've done me a service I can never repay. Look here, this is a forgery!"

"A forgery?" asked the amazed Freshman.

"Yes, that's never my signature to that promissory note! In fact, the whole note is forged. It's a little like my writing, but I know I never signed it. Say, I'm free, now!"

"You'd better tell me more about it," suggested our hero. "If I'm to have it out with Skeel for you, I'd better know all the facts."

"Sure. I'll tell you. It won't take long. I made an idiot of myself, to be brief. You know my father is well off, and he makes me a good allowance. One of his rules, though, and one I never broke but once, was never to gamble, and another was never to sign a note. I broke both.

"Last year when I was a Junior I got in with a fast set of fellows. We didn't do anything very bad, but one night there was a game of chance in one of the rooms. I was urged to play, and, not wanting to be a kill-joy, I foolishly agreed. I knew dad would never forgive me if he found it out, but I didn't think he would. He had said I would have to leave school, and go to work, if I gambled, or signed a note.

"Well, I lost, as most anyone will if he keeps it up long enough. I lost all my ready money, and I got in debt. I had no way of paying, and the Junior to whom I was indebted suggested that I give him my I. O. U. for the amount. I did, scribbling a promissory note on a piece of paper. The sum was quite large, and I see now what a chump I was. But I expected to be able to pay in time, and the fellow said there was no hurry.

"But when my next allowance came I went out on a lark, and we did some damage that we had to pay for. This took all the cash I had, and I owed more. I dared not ask for additional money, for I did not want to explain to dad how foolish I had been on two occasions. I went to the Junior, told him my predicament, and he kindly offered to wait for his debt, though the note was overdue.

"Then, most unexpectedly, this Junior's father died, and left him a lot of money. He left school in a hurry to arrange his affairs, and go abroad. The night before he left he wrote me a letter saying he had destroyed the promissory note, and said that I need not pay it, as it was a foolish debt at best.

"That made me happy until all at once the storm broke. Just before the close of school last term Professor Skeel sent for me. He told me he had a note of mine, and demanded payment. I was dumbfounded, and said I didn't know what he meant.

"He explained that before leaving, this junior, whose name I won't mention, had sold my promissory note to him, and that as he now owned it I must pay it to him. I said he was mistaken, and told about the letter I had."

"Why didn't you show it to him?" asked Tom. "That would have been good evidence."

"Very foolishly I had destroyed it as soon as I read of my release from the obligation. I did not want a scrap of paper around to remind me of it. So I had no proof, and Skeel only laughed at me. He said he held the note, and he showed it to me hastily, but I thought it was the real thing. He threatened, if I did not pay, to tell dad, and I knew what that meant, for, somehow, Skeel had learned about the game of chance.

"And that was my trouble. It's been hanging over me since last term and Skeel has been at me several times this term to pay up. He's been putting the screws on harder and harder, and today was the last day. If I couldn't pay he was to send word to dad, and demand the money from him. I did try to raise the cash to settle, and I've paid something on account, but I never could raise enough, for something always seemed to happen to use up my allowance, and I had no good excuse for asking for more."

"Why didn't you write to this Junior, asking if it was true that he had destroyed your note, as he said in his letter?" Tom inquired.

"I did, but I never could reach him. He went traveling in Europe. But it's all right now. I see the whole game. The Junior did tear up my note, but probably Skeel found the pieces, somehow. He made a forged copy of the note, enlarged the amount, forged my name to it, and the Junior's endorsement, and relied on my fear of publicity to make me pay. But I can now see that this is a fake!" and Bruce held up the document.

"Then the sooner we tell Skeel so to his face the better," said Tom, firmly. "Come on, we'll beard the tyrant in his den!"

And they went.

"You sent for me, Professor Skeel," began Bruce, when he and Tom were admitted to the study of the unpleasant Latin teacher.

"I did, but I have no desire to see this young man!" and he glared at Tom. "I demand that he withdraw at once."

"And I refuse!" exclaimed Tom. "I am here to represent Mr. Bennington, as—er—a sort of counsel."

"Then he has told you of his folly, eh?" sneered the professor. "There is no longer need for me to keep quiet about it. Are you ready to pay that note, Bennington, or shall I inform your father about your debts of honor? Remember I came into possession of the note honestly, as the third party, and the law will recognize my claim. You are not a minor, and you can not plead that. I bought the note from the student to whom you gave it. Now, are you ready to pay, or shall I expose you?"

"I am not going to pay," said Bruce, quietly.

"Then I'll disgrace you!" stormed Mr. Skeel.

"Have you the note in question?" asked Tom, quietly.

"Yes, but what is that to you? I can produce it when the time comes," and the professor tapped a black wallet lying on the table before him. It was the one Tom had found and returned.

"You need not trouble," said our hero quietly. "We can produce the note now. Here it is—the forged note!" and he held it in view, but safely out of reach of the professor, who had sprung to his feet in rage and amazement.

"Wha—what!" he cried. "Where—where did you get that?"

Hurriedly, and with trembling hands, he began searching through the wallet.

"It was there—it's here now," said Tom, quietly. "And if you make any more threats, or attempt in any way to annoy my friend here, I shall lay the whole matter before Doctor Meredith," went on the calm Freshman. "I don't know but it is my duty to do it anyhow," he added. "Forging notes and names is a serious crime."

Professor Skeel sank back in his chair, his face the color of chalk. His lips moved, but, for a moment, no sound came forth. Then he hoarsely whispered:

"Don't—don't expose me—I—I'll apologize. It was all—all a mistake. I—I—!"

He faltered, and Tom, not wishing to prolong the unpleasant scene, said to Bruce:

"Come."

The two walked out, silently, Tom handing the forged note to his friend. No one had a claim on him now.

"Tom Fairfield, you have saved me from disgrace!" said Bruce feelingly, and the two clasped hands in a firm grip.

CHAPTER XXV

A MISSING PROFESSOR

"Young gentlemen," began Doctor Meredith, as he faced the assembled Freshmen class in the chapel, where he had requested that they meet him, "this is a solemn occasion. I hardly know what to say to you. Never, in the history of Elmwood Hall, have we gone through what has transpired in the last few days. We have never had a strike, nor an occasion for one. We have never had a burning in effigy.

"I am at a loss what to say. I have tried to sit as an impartial judge in this matter, and so far, I have to admit that there is some right on both sides, and a great deal of wrong on one side—which side is yet to be determined."

Tom wanted to say something, but he refrained. The doctor was speaking too solemnly to be interrupted.

"I have considered this matter from all standpoints," went on the head master, "and I have tried to see my duty. I want to do what is right by all. For that purpose I have asked you to meet here, and I will now go a step further and will send for Professor Skeel. Perhaps, when we have a mutual conference, all differences will be explained, a new system can be devised and all will go on peacefully and quietly, as it always has at Elmwood Hall.

"I will ask our worthy janitor, Mr. Demosthenes Miller to step over to Professor Skeel's house, and request him to come here."

It was about an hour after Tom's dramatic interview with the Latin instructor. Our hero and Bruce had parted, Tom to go to Latin class, and, later, with all the Freshmen in that division, to attend the special meeting.

While the janitor was gone there was a painful silence. Then the footsteps of the returning messenger were heard. He came in alone.

"Is Professor Skeel coming?" asked Doctor Meredith curiously.

"No, sir, he is not," replied the janitor with a respectful bow.

"Why not?" and Doctor Meredith was plainly surprised.

"Because, Doctor Meredith, Professor Skeel has gone."

"Gone?"

"Yes, sir. Disappeared—vanesco as the classic Latin puts it. His servant just informed me that the professor packed up a few of his belongings, and went to town to catch a train. He will have his other things sent after him. So he will not be here. He also left word that he would not come back."

For a moment there was a silence. Then came a long breath of relief from the students. It was echoed by Doctor Meredith.

"This—er—this—rather simplifies matters," he said, a bit nervously. "I had it in mind to have Professor Skeel beg your pardon, and you, as a class, to beg his. Then matters would have gone on as before. But this simplifies matters. Professor Skeel, it seems, is no longer a member of the faculty of Elmwood Hall. I do not understand it, but I fear he has left for good."

"And I know it—I don't fear it," murmured Tom. "I'm glad of it, too. It saves me the disagreeable duty of branding him as a forger. All's well that ends well? I suppose."

"The purpose of this meeting having been accomplished," went on Doctor Meredith, "you may consider yourselves excused. You will report for Latin recitation to Professor Hammond, until further notice, and I will engage a new classical professor as soon as possible."

"Three cheers for Doctor Meredith!"

"Three more for Professor Hammond!"

"Three big ones for the Freshmen class," called Tom, when the first two had been given.

"And three cheers for Tom Fairfield, the best leader in Elmwood Hall!" shouted Jack Fitch, swinging his cap.

That the roof remained on the chapel after all that excitement speaks a good word for the workmen who placed it there. Certainly such cheering was never before heard in the old school.

"No more Skeel!" exulted Jack, as he walked out of chapel, his arm linked in Tom's.

"Nothing but fun from now on," declared Tom, "and it will soon be spring and baseball."

"What are you going to do this vacation?"

"I don't know. I've got to wait and see how dad and mother make out in Australia, I suppose. I must write and tell them all that happened here."

What Tom did when school closed may be learned by reading the next volume of this series, to be called, "Tom Fairfield at Sea; or, The Wreck of the Silver Star."

"And so Skeel forged that note?" asked Jack, when he and his chum were in their room that night.

"Yes, it was a rank copy of Bruce's signature. And he had raised the amount, too. I guess he was after money, all right."

"I wonder where he went?"

"Far enough off, I imagine. He'll never trouble Elmwood Hall again."

"Nor Bruce Bennington, either."

And this was so. Bruce was a different lad, from then on. His face was always smiling, as it had been before his trouble.

"I never can thank you, Tom, for what you did for me," he said. "Only for you Skeel would have carried out his threat, and his forgery never would have been discovered in time to prevent my disgrace. But I've made a clean breast of it to dad, and though he gave me a hard calling down, he's forgiven me. Oh, I feel so glad!"

"And so do I," added Tom. "We're going to have a new Latin prof. I understand. A jolly young fellow."

"That's good. Here comes Demy. I wonder what he wants?" spoke Bruce, as the studious janitor approached, with a book as usual.

"Well, what is it?" asked the Senior.

"I fear I have made a grave mistake," said Mr. Miller. "In announcing the disappearance of Professor Skeel the other day I used the Latin word *vanesco*. I see now that I used the wrong tense. Will you kindly set me right."

"Demy!" exclaimed Tom, "if you will kindly follow the example of Professor Skeel, and vamoose, it will be all the same. We'll give you a Latin lesson later. And, in the meanwhile, here is a dollar to buy a dictionary," and Tom passed over a bill to the man who was always a friend to the students.

As for Professor Skeel he was not heard of again for some time. But the lads of Elmwood Hall did not care. They had Tom Fairfield, who became more of a leader than ever after his successful strike. As for Sam Heller, he led a miserable life as a Freshman—ignored by nearly all.

"Come on in to town," invited Bruce that night. "I'll treat you fellows to a good feed, Tom. And I've fixed it with Merry, so we won't have to hurry back."

"Good!" exclaimed our hero, and on his way with his chums to a good time, we will say good-bye to him for a time.

THE END

Milton Keynes UK
Ingram Content Group UK Ltd.
UKHW020840260624
444769UK00011B/397